Alexander McCall Smith is the author of
the bestselling No. 1 Ladies' Detective
Agency series. He has written over thirty
books for young readers, including two
other School Ship *Tobermory* adventures.

Iain McIntosh's illustrations have won
awards in the worlds of advertising, design
and publishing. He has illustrated many
of Alexander McCall Smith's books.

THE RACE TO KANGAROO CLIFF

Alexander McCall Smith

Illustrated by
Iain McIntosh

First published in 2018 by
BC Books, an imprint of Birlinn Limited
West Newington House
10 Newington Road
Edinburgh
EH9 1QS

www.bcbooksforkids.co.uk

ISBN: 978 1 78027 453 9

British Library Cataloguing-in-Publication Data
A catalogue record for this book is available
from the British Library

Typeset by Mark Blackadder

MIX
Paper from
responsible sources
FSC® C117931

Printed and bound by MBM SCS Ltd, East Kilbride

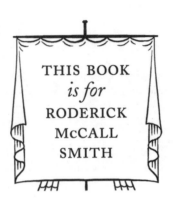

THIS BOOK
is for
RODERICK
McCALL
SMITH

ARCTIC

SCOTLAND

NORTH AMERICA

EUROPE

ASIA

Atlantic Ocean

AFRICA

Pacific Oc

Pacific Ocean

SOUTH AMERICA

The route from Scotland

Indian Ocean

AUSTRALIA

The Roaring Forties

ANTARCTIC

The Voyages of
SCHOOL SHIP
TOBERMORY
SCOTLAND to
AUSTRALIA
and
THE RACE
TO KANGAROO
CLIFF

Indian
Ocean

Route from Scotland

The Roaring Forties

CHAPTER 1

An unusual rescue

"Iceberg ahead!"

They were just two words, but they were enough to make the hairs on the back of Ben MacTavish's neck stand on end.

It was Badger Tomkins who had called out the warning. Ben and Badger shared a cabin on board the School Ship *Tobermory*, and they were good friends. When Badger gave his warning they were both on watch duty, their job being to look out for anything that could imperil the ship. Since they were sailing in the southern oceans, not far from Antarctica, ice was high on the list of dangers.

They were standing together at the prow, the very front of the ship. Above and behind them, secured to the towering masts, was the rigging and the great expanse of sails that drove them on their course. The wind was light, although it had blown strongly earlier that morning, and the ship was travelling slowly. That was just as well, as the last thing you want to do is to find yourself going too fast when there are icebergs about.

Ben strained his eyes. The early morning fog, thick and clammy like a cold white soup all around them, made it impossible to see very far. "Are you sure?" he asked his friend.

Badger nodded. "It was over there," he said, pointing to the bank of swirling fog. "The fog's hiding it now, but I'm sure it's there." He paused. "Or pretty sure."

"One-hundred-per-cent sure?" Ben pressed him.

Badger hesitated. "Ninety per cent," he replied. "Or eighty ..."

"Should we tell the Captain?" asked Ben.

Badger hesitated again. Nobody wanted a false alarm, but nobody liked crashing into an iceberg either. At length, he made up his mind. "I think we should warn him," he said. "It's always better to be safe than sorry. You go, Ben – I'll stay here and keep a look-out."

Captain Macbeth

Ben ran back towards the quarter-deck where Captain Macbeth, the skipper – and the school principal – was standing with some of the teachers and the student crew.

2

"Badger thinks he saw an iceberg," Ben informed him.

Captain Macbeth had been talking to Miss Worsfold, one of the teachers, but he cut off his conversation when he heard Ben's report.

"An iceberg, you say? Where?"

"Dead ahead," said Ben. "But a fog bank has swallowed it up and we can't see it any longer."

The Captain lost no time. Shouting out his instructions, he changed the course of the great ship, causing all but a few of the sails to lose their wind and flap limply about. Almost immediately, the ship was slowed down even more.

"You come with me," said Captain Macbeth to Ben. "We'll find out what's to be seen up there."

They joined Badger at his post.

"Any further sightings?" asked the Captain.

Badger was about to say, "No sir, nothing," but stopped himself. Ahead of them, off their starboard bow, the fog had cleared. And there, appearing from behind its swirling cover, was the steep-sided shape of an iceberg. It was not large by the standards of such things, but it was quite bulky enough to cause serious damage to any ship that collided with it.

"There it is!" shouted Badger.

"Yes," said the Captain. "I see it now."

Looking through his telescope, the Captain was able to tell that the iceberg was hardly moving and that if they kept on their current course they would not get too close to it.

"Well spotted," he said to Badger. "These things can easily sink a ship."

He looked again at the iceberg. Something had caught his attention.

"Well, well," said Captain Macbeth. "Now there's a sight you don't see very often."

Ben asked him what he had seen, and the Captain's answer was to pass him his telescope. "Take a look at the bottom right-hand corner," he said.

Ben focused the instrument. For the most part, all he could see was white, but then, as he adjusted the eyepiece, something else came into focus – something that was small and black and white. He blinked, and looked again: *Surely not*, he thought, and yet, as he looked again he realised that his first impression had been correct.

"It's a penguin," exclaimed Ben. "There's a little penguin on the iceberg."

The tiny, marooned penguin was standing on the very edge of the ice, looking back at him across the expanse of cold water.

By now they had been joined by others, who had been working nearby and had come to see what the excitement was all about. Poppy Taggart, who was a close friend of Ben's sister Fee, was there, as were their other friends, Angela Singh and Thomas Seagrape.

As the telescope was passed around, they all expressed surprise at seeing a penguin in such a lonely and improbable place.

"It can happen," said the Captain. "I've seen penguins trapped on ice floes before, so I suppose they can end up on icebergs too."

"But how?" asked Poppy.

The Captain explained. "It might have hopped up on it just before that chunk of ice separated itself," he said. "Then, before it knew it, the ice would have drifted off."

"Poor creature," said Thomas Seagrape. "It must be miles and miles from all the other penguins."

For a while there was silence. Ben imagined they were all thinking the same thing, but he was the one who finally put it into words. "Will it die?" he asked.

The Captain frowned. "I'm afraid it won't be able to survive much longer all by itself. So … well, yes, I'm sorry to say, it probably will die."

Again there was silence. The ship was moving very slowly and the ice was drifting along at much the same pace. For a while, at least, they and the little penguin were companions in the middle of this vast ocean.

It was Thomas Seagrape who spoke next. "Can't we rescue it?" he asked.

All eyes turned to Captain Macbeth. He looked at the students: it was clear that he was wrestling with a problem. They had a lengthy journey ahead of them and it would take at least an hour to lower a liberty boat – one of the *Tobermory*'s small rowing boats – and row over to the iceberg, rescue the penguin and bring it back to the ship. An hour may not seem like a long time, but when you are crossing a great ocean an hour's delay could mean that you miss the wind or wander off course.

And yet there are more important things in life than being on time.

"Are you really keen to do that?" asked the Captain.

The answer came in a chorus of voices which all said the same thing: "Yes!"

"In that case," said the Captain, giving his orders quickly, "Poppy, get a crew together to row over to the iceberg. Thomas, go and tell Miss Worsfold I'd like her to skipper the boat."

With a broad smile on his face, Thomas Seagrape saluted briskly and set off on his errand. For her part, Poppy immediately appointed Fee and Angela to her boat crew, along with Badger and Ben. They all then went off to fetch their lifejackets and their warmest sea clothing. Rowing up to an iceberg would be a chilly business, Poppy warned them. She had never done it herself, but just one glance in the direction of the great chunk of ice was enough to tell her that this was so.

Miss Worsfold spoke to them all before they climbed down the gangway to the liberty boat.

"We're setting out on a dangerous mission," she said. "I want everybody to be extra careful as the water round here is really cold. If anybody falls in, we'll be in real trouble. You don't have much time in water this cold before your muscles stop working. Does everybody understand that?"

They did.

"And another thing," said Miss Worsfold. "When we reach the iceberg, it might be very difficult to get onto it. Icebergs are slippery and you'll need to have a good sense of balance. I'll go myself, but I'll need a volunteer to come with me."

The teacher looked around her. "Poppy," she continued, "you'll have to stay on the boat, as you'll be in charge of the oars. Now, is there anybody here who's ever done any ice skating?"

Fee put up her hand. "I have, Miss Worsfold."

"Would you like to come with me, then?" asked Miss Worsfold. "You'll have developed a bit of balance on the ice rink."

Fee nodded. She was happy to assist, and she listened carefully as Miss Worsfold explained how she planned to catch the penguin. "They're very trusting birds," she said. "Usually you can walk right up to them. But we'll take a fishing net, just in case."

They were now ready to leave, and one by one they made their way down to the rowing boat that was bobbing up and down at the side of the *Tobermory*.

Above them, lining the ship's railings, were most of the other students. When the ship had slowed down they had realised that something was happening and they had all come to witness the rescue in progress. Although excited, they were quiet as they watched the boat, commanded by Miss Worsfold and rowed by Poppy and her crew, move away from the side of the *Tobermory*.

The iceberg had drifted a bit closer to the ship now, and it did not take them too long to row across to it.

"Ship oars!" commanded Poppy, when they were close enough.

This was the instruction to stop rowing, and it brought the small boat to a stop. Now they were within touching distance of the iceberg and Poppy was able to toss a rope across to its side. At the end of this rope was a small grappling hook that dug into the surface of the ice once the rope was given a tug. This anchored the boat and enabled Miss Worsfold and Fee to step out onto a flat section of the floating chunk of ice.

It was a tricky business walking towards the penguin, and once or twice Fee had to stretch out her arms on either side to regain her balance. The penguin was not far away, on a flat section of ice just above the surface of the water, and it watched them inquisitively as they approached.

"I don't think it's frightened," whispered Fee.

"Neither do I," agreed Miss Worsfold. "And I don't think we'll need our net."

They approached the marooned bird very slowly, Miss Worsfold holding out a hand towards it as if offering it food. Her hand was only a few inches away when there was a sudden splash in the water just beneath the place where the penguin was sitting. And at the same time, there was a loud noise – something between a bark and a snarl.

Miss Worsfold and Fee looked down into the water with horror. There, its head projecting from the water, was the largest seal either of them had ever seen. And as they stared at it, the seal opened its mouth to reveal a set of massive curved teeth.

Miss Worsfold acted instantly, pushing Fee back from the edge of the ice. Then, scooping up the surprised penguin, she shouted out to Fee to follow her back to the waiting boat as quickly as possible.

Once they reached the boat, Miss Worsfold passed the penguin to Poppy, who placed it carefully in the small wooden box they had brought to transport it. The penguin did not struggle, seeming to be quite happy to go along with this unexpected rescue.

As the boat made its way back to the *Tobermory*, they heard a loud cheer come across the water from the ship. Everybody on board had seen what had happened and was applauding the bravery of the rescue crew.

Miss Worsfold sat in the boat and wiped her brow. "That was a very narrow escape," she said, her voice revealing the fear she had just experienced. "That wasn't an ordinary seal, everybody – that was a leopard seal."

Fee shivered at the thought. They had been within striking distance of one of the most dangerous creatures in the sea – one which would be happy to make a meal of you if it found you in its waters. If they had waited a few seconds longer, it could have launched itself up out of the water and sunk its teeth into the nearest human leg. And if that had happened, the unfortunate victim would have been dragged down into the icy water below. It did not bear thinking about.

The Captain welcomed them back on board. His first officer, Mr Rigger, who also taught seamanship, was already preparing a small hutch for the penguin. This was placed near the stern, in a position where the penguin would get lots of fresh air and would be able to shelter from the wind. Cook had already found a couple of fresh fish that he had placed in a small bowl just inside the hutch. It was as fine a home as any penguin could hope for and was much better than the perilous sanctuary that the iceberg had provided.

Cook had also prepared a mug of warming hot chocolate for every member of the rescue crew. This

Cook

was served downstairs in the mess hall, and as they sipped at the welcome hot drink Miss Worsfold explained what had happened.

"I think the penguin had become a bit weak," she said. "He had been sitting on the iceberg, too frightened to dive for fish. And the reason he was frightened – well, we discovered that, didn't we, Fee?"

Fee shuddered at the memory of the leopard seal's great mouth with its wicked-looking teeth.

"You see," continued Miss Worsfold, "I think the penguin was not the only passenger on that iceberg."

Poppy drew in her breath. "You mean the seal lived on it too?"

Miss Worsfold nodded. "That leopard seal had probably decided to hitch a ride on the iceberg. It would have been all right, because seals are very efficient hunters and there would have been plenty of fish for it swimming around the ice below. But what it really wanted, I should think, was a tasty meal of penguin. And that was about to happen when we arrived."

"So you saved the penguin from becoming a meal for a leopard seal?" asked Badger.

Miss Worsfold said that this was so. "I think we were just in time," she said.

"I'm glad," said Badger. But then he thought of something. They could not keep the penguin on board forever – they would have to find a home for it. But they were not going to sail further south to Antarctica itself, so where would that home be?

Badger asked Miss Worsfold what they would do with the penguin. She confessed that she had not thought too much about that, but that she imagined there were zoos in Australia, where they were heading, that would be able to offer it a comfortable home. "It will get everything it needs," she said. "A pool to swim in, lots of fresh fish each day and, in hot weather, a refrigerated enclosure to spend the night in."

Miss Worsfold had a bit more to say about penguins – and about the other creatures that lived down at the cold ends of the world. "They're finding it a bit difficult these days," she said. "Polar ice caps are melting, and that causes all kinds of problems for them."

Poppy had read that polar bears in particular were suffering. "They don't have enough to eat," she said. "And they're getting caught on ice floes."

Miss Worsfold nodded sadly. "It's a very hard time for our fellow creatures," she said. "Not only for polar bears and penguins, but for elephants and wolves and tigers …"

"But at least we've saved one penguin," said Badger. "And that's a good thing, isn't it?"

Miss Worsfold looked a bit more cheerful. "You're right, Badger." She paused. "And would you like to be in charge of the penguin-feeding rota?"

Badger said he would, but only if Fee would be in charge with him. "She's the one who rescued him," he said. "With you, of course, Miss Worsfold," he quickly added.

Fee was happy to be involved. She would do Monday to Wednesday, while Badger would do Thursday to Saturday. Poppy could cover Sunday, if she agreed, which she did.

"That's all fixed then," said Miss Worsfold. "Speak to Cook about fish. There's plenty in the freezers so our penguin shouldn't go hungry." She paused, then continued. "Our penguin ... I think we'll have to find a name for him."

"Or her," said Poppy.

"Yes, I suppose we don't know right now whether it's male or female. But I think Cook will be able to tell us."

Fee was puzzled. "Cook? Does he know about penguins?"

"Not especially," said Miss Worsfold. "But he's always been a keen birdwatcher. He'll know."

"Couldn't we have a name that suited both a boy and a girl penguin?" asked Poppy.

"Such as?" asked Miss Worsfold. "Any ideas, anybody?"

Ben shouted out the first thing that came into his mind. "Feathers! How about Feathers?"

"That's great," said Poppy. "And it's accurate, isn't it? After all, you couldn't call a dog Feathers, could you?"

Everybody agreed that Feathers was a good name for the penguin and that it did not matter whether he was a he or she was a she. The important thing was that he (or she) had been saved from being a leopard seal's lunch.

That night, as Badger and Ben lay in their bunks after lights out, Badger asked Ben a question. "Would you prefer to be eaten by a shark or a seal, Ben?"

Ben replied that he did not think it would make much difference. "It would hurt pretty badly either way," he said.

"Or a whale?" Badger asked. "I wonder what it would be like to be swallowed by a whale."

"It would be very dark," said Ben. "But at least when the whale opened his mouth you could swim out again."

"I'd prefer not to get too close to any of those things," Badger mused. And then, remembering where the ship was headed, he asked Ben what were the things he hoped he would *not* meet in Australia.

"One of those very poisonous spiders you find there," said Ben in the darkness. "I don't much like the sound of them."

"Or a saltwater crocodile," suggested Badger. He had been reading about Australian wildlife and he had not liked what he had read about crocodiles. "It's the most aggressive crocodile in the world," he went on. "It will even chase you on land."

"I'll keep a good look-out," muttered Ben. He was beginning to feel sleepy and was not sure that he wanted to drop off with thoughts of crocodiles in his mind.

But Badger had more to say. "It doesn't matter if you keep a good look-out," he warned. "You can't see them, you know. They're just below the surface of the water, and you don't always notice them until it's too late."

"Oh, well …" Ben said. "You can't stop doing things just because of crocodiles …"

And with that he fell asleep and did not hear what else Badger had to say – which did not matter too much, as Badger himself was tired by now and had little to add about crocodiles or anything else.

CHAPTER 2

Where are we going next?

How was it that Ben and Fee and a large group of other young people should find themselves on a sailing ship on the far southern oceans rescuing – of all unlikely things – a stranded penguin? The answer to that is that they were at school, which is where just about everyone of their age has to spend a lot of time. But in their case their school happened to be a ship.

The *Tobermory*, in fact, is one of the best-known school ships in the world. It is based in Scotland, on the island of Mull, but it takes young people from many different countries. What each one has in common is the desire to learn about ships and the sea while at the same time doing all the usual things you do at school. This means that it is easier – if they want it – to become sailors when they grow up and have to get a job.

Ben and Fee MacTavish were twins who had just celebrated their thirteenth birthday, though, as Fee liked to point out, she was in fact two minutes older then her brother. They had joined the *Tobermory*

Ben MacTavish

because their parents, who were famous marine scientists, had to be away from home a great deal. This meant that they could not go to an ordinary school, but had to find a school where they could stay while their parents were away in their research submarine.

"I'm glad we chose the *Tobermory*," said Fee to her brother. "Not all schools can be as much fun as this."

Ben agreed. "I love being here," he said. "I like everything about it."

And he did. He liked the Captain – Captain Macbeth – who had a friendly dog called Henry. He liked the Captain's assistant, Mr Rigger, with his famous moustache that could act as a weather vane and would let you know where the wind was coming from.

Fee MacTavish

Mr Rigger

He liked Matron, who had been a famous diver in the Olympics before she met and married Cook, who made possibly the best sausages in the northern hemisphere. And of course he liked all the friends he had made since he joined the school, most of whom were members of the same deck as he was.

The living quarters of the *Tobermory* were divided into three decks – Upper, Middle and Lower. Each had a senior student – the Deck Prefect – who was meant to keep order. Poppy was Head Prefect of Ben's deck, the Middle Deck. She was popular, and did the job well, unlike William Edward Hardtack, Head Prefect of the Upper Deck, who was more disliked than respected.

Ben's main friend was Badger. While Ben came from Scotland, Badger was an American boy whose parents lived in New York. His father worked there

Matron

Badger

and was extremely busy – so busy that he seemed to have little time to spend with his son. This saddened Badger. You only have one father in this life, and it seemed to Badger that he would grow up without ever seeing much of his. But he never complained. Badger was like that – he looked on the positive side of things.

Ben liked Badger's cheerful attitude and his special talent. That talent was the ability, when he was speaking to you, to make you feel that of all the people in the world, you were the one he really wanted to be talking to. Ben had noticed that there are some people who let their eyes wander when they speak to you and never look at you directly. This makes you think they would rather be speaking to somebody else, and not you. Badger never did that.

Ben's sister Fee had a special friend in Poppy, who came from Australia. If you asked Fee what she liked about Poppy, she would say that she really appreciated the way that Poppy did things. If you asked her to explain further, she would probably say something like this: "Lots of people who are good at things make you

feel small. They push you aside and do things much better than you can. Poppy never does that. She shows you how to do something and then you do it together. That makes you feel proud to have done something that you otherwise might not have been able to do."
Another way of putting all

Poppy

that would be to say: *Poppy is helpful* – which she certainly was.

There were others too in this group of friends from Middle Deck. There was Thomas Seagrape, who

Thomas Seagrape

came from Jamaica, an island in the Caribbean Sea. Thomas knew a lot about the sea because his mother was the skipper of a ship that ran between Jamaica and nearby islands. Ben liked him because of his smile and his kindness. Thomas was also brave – which is a quality Ben admired.

Tanya Herring

Then there was Tanya Herring, who had been a stowaway and who had been allowed to stay on board because of the Captain's good heart. If Captain Macbeth had sent her home, she would have had to return to her wicked uncle and aunt who ran dog kennels in Scotland and who had made her work all hours of the day. Tanya's father was a sailor too, but Tanya had lost touch with him and hoped one day that she would find him somewhere on the world's great oceans. So far she had had no luck in that quest.

There was Angela Singh, who came from India, and who was good at subjects like mathematics and history but who tended to be a bit nervous about everything else. But little by little, Angela was becoming more courageous, and was encouraged in this by Poppy.

"Don't think too much about what might go wrong," Poppy advised her. "Just take a deep breath and do what you have to do. You may find it much easier than you thought."

Those were the main friends. But there were others

– people who were not so friendly. If you have a large group of people, then you are more or less bound to have one or two who are not so nice. In this case it was three, and their names were William Edward Hardtack, who was famous for sneering at others, Geoffrey Shark, who was extremely pleased both

Angela Singh

with himself and his fancy hairstyle, which was remarkably like the fin of a shark, and Maximilian Flubber, whose ears flapped backwards and forwards whenever he told a lie, which was quite often.

There was not much anybody could do about this group.

"They're like bad weather," said Poppy. "You have to put up with bad weather, and so you have to put up with Hardtack and Co. It's just the way it is."

"They're not going to spoil anything for me," said Fee.

"Nor for me," agreed Angela.

But that was easier said than done. The trouble with people like Hardtack, Shark and Flubber was that spoiling things for other people was exactly what they liked to do.

The voyage to Australia came a short while after the *Tobermory* had returned from sailing around the Caribbean. That had been a particularly exciting trip, and most people were happy to have a bit of a rest after it. But once they had returned to Tobermory, the port on the island of Mull after which the ship was named, the students began wondering what would be their next destination.

There were plenty of rumours.

"I've heard we're going to Hong Kong," said Badger one morning at breakfast.

Poppy looked surprised. "Oh yes?" she said. "Well, I heard it was going to be South America – Chile in fact."

"No," said Tanya. "I saw Matron studying a chart of the seas around India. I bet it's India, because why else would Matron be looking at that chart?"

Thomas Seagrape had an altogether different theory. "I heard Cook talking about how to get to San Francisco. He said something about the Panama Canal. So I think we're going all the way to the west coast of America."

Poppy laughed. "Let's face it," she said, "we've all heard different things and the *Tobermory* can't be going to all those places. Why don't we …"

"Ask the Captain?" continued Fee.

"Exactly," said Poppy.

The opportunity to do that arose sooner than they

thought. It came at dinner time shortly after, when Captain Macbeth came to the mess hall to address the whole school and at the end asked whether anybody had any questions.

At first everybody was silent. Then a hand went up. It was Badger's.

"Yes, Tomkins," said the Captain. "What is it?"

Badger stood up and cleared his throat. He tried not to look in Hardtack's direction, as he could imagine he would be smirking.

"I was wondering," began Badger. "I mean, quite a few of us were wondering where we're going next."

Captain Macbeth smiled. "Oh you were, were you?" he said.

Badger nodded. "It's just that … it's just that it's good to know where you're going to be."

The Captain considered this. Turning to Mr Rigger, who was standing at his side, he said, "That seems perfectly reasonable, wouldn't you say, Mr Rigger?"

Mr Rigger nodded. "I'd say so, Captain."

The atmosphere in the mess hall was electric with anticipation.

"It's going to be in the southern hemisphere," said Captain Macbeth.

Mr Rigger nodded. "Southern hemisphere," he echoed.

The Captain was enjoying himself. "And I can reveal to you that it's a continent."

Hardtack called out: "Antarctica."

The Captain shook his head. "No, not Antarctica."

Fee was particularly good at geography, and realised that with Antarctica ruled out, there was not much choice. She put up her hand.

"Are we going to Australia?" she asked.

"Yes," said the Captain. "That's exactly where we're going," before adding, "and we shall be leaving next week."

Captain Macbeth then went on to explain why Australia had been chosen as their destination. "Australia's a wonderful country," he began. "It's worth going there just to see it. But there's something more. There's going to be a Tall Ships race out there, starting at Cairns in Queensland and running all the way up round the tip of the continent."

At this announcement a loud cheer rang through the mess hall. A number of people had been hoping that Australia would be the *Tobermory*'s next destination, but had thought it would be considered too far away from Scotland.

There was one person who was especially pleased by this news, and that was Poppy. She came from Alice Springs, right in the middle of Australia, where her parents ran a sheep farm. If the ship called in at Sydney or Melbourne, she was sure her mother and father would make the long journey to meet them. She would then be able to show them round her school, which she had been keen to do ever since she started there. And she liked the idea, too, of being able to introduce her friends to some of the things that in her mind made Australia one of the best places on Earth. She would show them kangaroos and wallabies; she would take them camping in the bush and brew up a pot of tea in her billy can; she would take them to see people who knew how to throw a boomerang properly; she would take them to a beach where they could go surfing. There was so much she could show them.

Not everybody was happy. As they filed out of the mess hall, Poppy found herself close to William Edward Hardtack and his friends. "Boring, boring," muttered Hardtack. "Who wants to go to a place that's flat and empty? Who wants to go somewhere like that?"

"Not me," said Geoffrey Shark.

"Nor me," added Maximilian Flubber, his ears beginning to twitch.

Poppy felt her cheeks flush with rage at the insult. How dare Hardtack, who knew next to nothing about anything, and even less about Australia, say things like that?

"Excuse me," she hissed. "Have you ever been to Australia, Hardtack? Or you, Shark? Or Flubber, you too – have you ever been there?"

"Never wanted to," snapped Hardtack.

"Too many people like *you* there," said Shark.

This made his two accomplices laugh.

"You're very ignorant," said Poppy, struggling to control herself. "Australia is a terrific country. And if you don't want to see it, I can tell you that Australia doesn't want to see you either."

Chuckling over what they thought of as their witty remarks, the three boys disappeared down the corridor.

"Ignore them," said Angela Singh, who had overheard this exchange. "They're stupid. I can't wait to see Australia – and I think just about everybody else on board feels the same. It sounds like a fabulous place."

"It is," said Poppy. "And I know you won't be disappointed once you get there."

"I'm sure I won't," said Angela. She had a question, though, but she could not quite bring herself to ask it. She wanted to know about spiders and snakes, but she knew that everybody was aware of her worries about such things, so she said nothing.

Poppy looked at her friend and smiled. She could guess what Angela was thinking.

"And you mustn't worry about …" She lowered her voice. "About funnel-web spiders and so on. Australia's a pretty safe place, you know."

Angela swallowed hard. "Oh, I wasn't worried," she said.

"Of course you weren't," said Poppy kindly. "You're really going to like Australia, Angela – I'm sure of that."

CHAPTER 3

Flubber slips

They had to get to Australia first, and that involved a long sea voyage. Captain Macbeth explained it all to them on the day before they were due to weigh anchor and set off.

"As you know," he said, "Australia is on the other side of the world from Scotland, and that means it will take us at least eight weeks to get there."

Everybody looked at one another as they absorbed this news.

"Eight weeks at sea!" Fee whispered to Poppy. She wondered what it would be like being at sea for that long. And would their supplies of food hold out for such a length of time, or would they have to catch fish to keep them going?

Poppy smiled. "We'll get used to it. And time will pass quickly enough – it always does when you're on a ship."

The Captain went on to describe their route. They would take the same course used by sailing ships in the days of clippers – the fast ships that sailed between

Britain and Australia back in the eighteen-hundreds. That would take them down the middle of the Atlantic Ocean, past the bulge of South America and then straight across to Australia.

"The winds we want to catch down there," Captain Macbeth went on, "are called the Roaring Forties."

Some people gasped at this. The Roaring Forties! Miss Worsfold had said something about these winds, Fee remembered, in one of her geography lessons. The name said it all. The 'Forties' referred to the latitude of these winds – how far they are south of the equator – and 'Roaring', well, that is what high winds do: they roar. For a moment she imagined what these winds would do to Mr Rigger's famous moustache, which would probably look something like this …

Mr Rigger took over from Captain Macbeth to explain that the further south they went, the shorter the route would be – and the better the winds. "But," he added, "going that far south increases the chance of finding ice. So we shall have to be careful."

"Extremely careful," agreed the Captain. "Remember the *Titanic*."

That is not a name that sailors like to think about too much. The *Titanic* was a famous passenger liner that hit an iceberg on her maiden voyage and sank as a result. People had boasted that she was unsinkable, but that had been proved to be untrue: the *Titanic* had gone to the bottom of the sea, along with most of her unfortunate passengers and crew. Hitting an iceberg is just like sailing straight into the side of a mountain, and few ships would survive that undamaged.

These warnings, though, did not spoil the excitement, and over the few days that remained before they set off, the mood on the *Tobermory* was one of excitement. There was much to do, of course, and all classes were suspended while the ship was prepared. Everything was washed, polished and double-checked. Ropes were coiled, rigging tightened and decks scrubbed until not a speck of dirt remained, and then scrubbed again. Supplies were brought aboard from onshore: bags of rice and flour, crates of tinned beans, sausages, sacks of potatoes, great blocks of butter – everything that would be needed to make three meals a day for everyone for eight weeks.

"There are no shops at sea," Cook was fond of pointing out, "so if we run out of anything, we can't just nip out and buy it!"

At last everything was packed and the *Tobermory* was ready to leave the small harbour that shared her name.

On the morning of their departure, Badger was already washed and dressed by the time Ben woke up. As a special treat for his friend, Badger had gone off to the mess hall, where tea was served from a large urn, and brought a mug back for Ben.

"Time to wake up," he said once he was back in their cabin. "And here's your mug of tea in bed – I mean, in hammock."

Ben rubbed the sleep from his eyes and then accepted the mug of steaming tea.

"You're really kind, Badge," he said, as he took his first sip of the hot liquid.

"That's what friends are for," Badger replied, smiling. "Besides, I woke up at least an hour ago and was just too excited to go back to sleep."

"I think I was dreaming about the Roaring Forties when you woke me up," said Ben. "I dreamt there were massive waves and the ship was tilting right over."

Badger smiled again. "That's what it's going to be like," he said. "Only it won't be a dream."

They sailed down the coast of Ireland, through the Irish Sea and then out into the open Atlantic. The Atlantic is one of the great oceans of the world, and only seagoing ships, tough and well-made, can stand some of the conditions found there. The famous Atlantic swell is one of the hardest tests awaiting sailors – these are vast mountains of water that travel from one side of the ocean to the other, lifting up and then dropping whatever floats on them. Then there are the waves themselves, which can be higher than a house and sometimes break with immense force, crushing whatever is below them under tons of cascading water.

On the *Tobermory*, new rules were issued by the Captain.

"When you're on deck," he announced to the crew as they left the protective cover of the Irish coast, "if the sea is rough, you must – and I mean really must – have lifelines clipped on to your lifejackets at all times. Anybody found on deck in such conditions without a lifeline will have to answer to Mr Rigger and me. And we shall not be lenient – I can assure you of that. Isn't that so, Mr Rigger?"

Mr Rigger nodded gravely. "I've seen people swept off deck in a big sea," he warned. "If they'd been wearing lifelines, they would still be with us." He paused. "Instead of which, they're down below in Davy Jones' Locker now."

"That means they drowned," whispered Poppy.

Ben gave an involuntary shiver. He could hardly imagine what it must be like to be swept overboard and to realise that you might not be rescued. The trouble with going overboard in high seas is that you can very quickly disappear behind a large wave and people on board might not spot you. He shivered again. He would wear his lifeline – he was certain of that.

For their first few days in the Atlantic, the ocean behaved itself. Although there was a small swell, the sea was calm and everyone was wondering what all those dire warnings had been about. But then, on the third day out, they awoke to a sky of dark grey clouds. The wind was rising now and it was beginning to whistle through the rigging, making a long, low moaning sound, rather like an animal in distress.

The Captain gave the order for lifejackets to be worn and for lifelines to be attached. Mr Rigger checked everybody before they went on deck, sending anybody who had forgotten to put on a lifejacket back down below to find one. Up on deck, it was the turn of Poppy, Fee and Angela to be on watch. Poppy was at the helm and Fee was standing immediately beside her. Angela was in charge of watching the compass, giving Poppy a warning when she needed to steer the ship back on course.

It all happened very quickly – as things at sea so

often do. One moment everything is all right and going smoothly, and the next something dreadful has occurred and there is a full-scale emergency.

Poppy had spotted Flubber crossing the deck, on his way to join Shark and Hardtack, who were on starboard watch at the time.

"Flubber!" shouted Poppy. "Your lifejacket! Where is it? The Captain says we're all to wear lifejackets and have lifelines until this wind dies down."

Flubber halted in his tracks and stared at Poppy. Then, cupping his hands so that he could be heard against the wailing of the wind, he shouted his response: "Mind your own business!"

Poppy felt the anger well up within her. It *was* her business, because if Flubber were to be washed overboard when she was at the helm, she would have to steer the ship round to rescue him. No, she had every right to tell him to put on his lifejacket.

"Flubber," she said, "I'm at the helm and I'm telling you – put on your lifejacket!"

But Flubber simply laughed what, if things had turned out just a little differently, might have been the very last laugh of his life.

Flubber continued to saunter across the deck and did not see the huge wave building up off the side of the *Tobermory*. This was a rogue wave – the name given to a large wave that comes from an unexpected direction. A large enough rogue wave can sink a ship if it hits it in the wrong place. This wave did not do that, but it did break over the deck of the *Tobermory*, flooding it badly, washing various ropes and buckets over the side and into the angry sea below.

Shocked and surprised, Flubber was knocked off his feet as well and carried at great speed across the deck by the surge of water. He might very easily have been washed off the deck altogether and into the open sea had he not managed to grab onto the railings as he headed off the side. This left him half on the ship and half off it, clinging with all his strength, shouting for help at the top of his voice.

The crash of the waves and the howling of the wind drowned his cries, with the result that his friends Hardtack and Shark did not hear him. Nor did they see him, as they were looking out to sea in the opposite direction when all this happened. Poppy saw him, though, as did Fee, and they both gave a shout.

"Flubber! Flubber's going overboard!"

Not far away, Badger heard them. Looking up, on the other side of the deck he saw two hands gripping the railing, hanging on for dear life. Without a second's hesitation, Badger launched himself across the deck, wading through the last of the draining water to reach his imperilled shipmate. As Badger reached the side, Flubber was just about to let go – it can be very hard to support yourself like that. Fortunately, he still had a few ounces of strength left in him,

and this kept him from disappearing into the sea.

"Hold on!" shouted Badger as he took hold of Flubber's wrists. "I'm going to pull you back on board."

Badger tensed his muscles and then, with a supreme effort, gave as strong a yank as he could manage. This brought Flubber back onto the deck, wet right through, panting and spluttering every bit as much as if he were a fish hauled from the water.

Mr Rigger appeared. He had heard Poppy and Fee shouting and had come up on deck to see what was happening. Now, peering down at the sodden bundle that was Maximilian Flubber, he spoke firmly to the rescued boy. "Why no lifejacket, Mr Flubber?" he asked. "Didn't you hear what the Captain said?"

Flubber sat up and tried to wipe the salt water out of his eyes.

"I was just putting it on, Mr Rigger," he said. "Then this great big wave came and washed it out of my hands. I promise you that's what happened."

It was a lie, of course – Flubber was always telling lies – and his ears started to wiggle, as they always did when he lied.

"Is that so?" Mr Rigger asked Badger. "Did you see all this, Tomkins?"

Badger did not know what to say. Nobody likes telling tales, but at the same time nobody – except people like Flubber – wants to tell a direct lie. The problem was, of course, that he had not seen Flubber with his lifejacket.

"Well?" said Mr Rigger. He stared at Badger, waiting for the boy to answer, but Badger simply remained silent.

Flubber spoke. "Can I get up, Mr Rigger?" he asked. "I've got water in my ears and I need to get it out."

Mr Rigger sighed. "Yes, I suppose so, but listen to me, Flubber. You could have been drowned right before our eyes. Never, ever forget your lifejacket when the wind and the sea are in this mood. Remember that."

Flubber rose to his feet and Mr Rigger went back below.

"I hope you're all right," said Badger. "That was a close thing."

Flubber was dismissive. "I was never going to drown," he said. "People like me don't drown, you know. It's you guys who drown because you're useless swimmers."

Badger ignored this provocation. He knew there was no point arguing with people like Flubber. Rather, he would give a full report to the Captain, so that he might know exactly what was going on. If he wanted to punish Flubber, then that was the Captain's business.

By now, Hardtack had come across to find out what had happened.

"You okay, Flubs?" asked Hardtack. "These people bothering you?"

Badger drew in his breath. The sheer cheek of Hardtack's comment astonished him. He had saved Flubber's life, and now Hardtack was beginning to threaten him.

Flubber looked down at the deck. He did not look at Badger as he spoke. "It's all right, Tacky," he said, "I'm fine."

Hardtack gave Badger a warning glance and then led Flubber back to where Shark was standing. Badger went to join Poppy and Fee, who were still standing at the helm and who were eager to hear exactly what had happened.

"I can't believe it," said Poppy. "Flubber should have thanked you for saving his life."

Poppy was right, of course – Flubber had not said so much as the smallest thank you. But that evening, when they were all in the mess hall having their dinner, Flubber appeared behind Badger's chair and whispered something in his ear.

"I meant to say thank you," he said. "And I would have said it if it hadn't been for …" He left the sentence unfinished.

"If it hadn't been for what?" asked Badger.

Flubber looked nervously in the direction of the table where Hardtack and Shark were sitting. "If it hadn't been for Tacky," he said. "He didn't want me to."

For a while, Badger said nothing. But Flubber's words made him think. Some people appear bad, but maybe they are really not quite as bad as you think they are. Sometimes they are under the influence of some stronger, nastier person. Perhaps Flubber was like that. He was weak and Hardtack was strong, and Hardtack knew that he could bully him into doing his bidding.

Badger looked into Flubber's eyes. He saw weakness there – and fear.

"It's all right, Flubber," he said quietly. "I know it can't be easy being Hardtack's friend."

Flubber looked back at him with gratitude. "Thanks, Badger," he said, his voice so low as to be almost inaudible. "I'll remember that."

CHAPTER 4

Surf dog

Four weeks later, as they sailed off the coast of South America, the winds died down and the sea became much friendlier. Instead of huge rollers travelling from horizon to horizon, there were now small, well-behaved waves that could barely be felt on a big ship like the *Tobermory*. It was warmer, too. The wind further north had been cool and sometimes even cold. Now it was like the breath of a large animal on the skin – a comfortable feeling that would never make you shiver or seek shelter. The sun too shone without interruption from dawn until dusk, dancing on the surface of the water with golden shoes.

Now that there was less work to do on deck, ordinary lessons had begun again in the classrooms down below. Miss Worsfold started her geography lessons and introduced everybody to currents and the effect they had not only on ships but also on the weather.

"There's a very important current called *El Niño*," she explained. "It flows off the west coast of South

America, but it's responsible for droughts and floods all over the world."

She drew a picture on the board. "That's a big current," she said. "There are smaller, weaker currents all around us, and if you're a sailor you should know about them. Why?" she asked.

Miss Worsfold

Angela Singh put up her hand. "Because they can give you a free ride," she said. "A boat can go much faster if a current helps it along."

Miss Worsfold nodded. "Or more slowly," she said, "if it goes against the current. That's more like walking uphill."

Currents came into other lessons too, such as the maths class that Mr Rigger taught each morning.

"Let's imagine," he began, "that there's a current of 1.2 knots going east to west. Let's imagine too that you're on a ship following a course west to east – that is, against the current. The wind is pushing you along at six knots an hour and you sail for five hours." He paused, looking out over the heads of the class. "How far will you have travelled at the end of those five hours?"

Ben looked at Badger, who frowned. Badger was good at doing this sort of calculation. "Come on, Badge," he whispered. "You can work this out with your eyes shut."

Badger did close his eyes, but only briefly. Then he opened them and raised his hand.

"Twenty-four miles," he said.

"Wrong," said Mr Rigger.

Badger looked puzzled. "But six multiplied by five is thirty. Then you take away 1.2 multiplied by five, which is six, and you get twenty-four miles."

Mr Rigger shook a finger. "You're forgetting something."

Poppy suddenly realised what it was that Badger had forgotten. "*Nautical* miles!" she burst out.

Mr Rigger clapped his hands together. "Exactly," he said. "A mile is 1,760 yards or 1,609.34 metres. A *nautical* mile, which is the same as a knot is …"

"One thousand eight hundred and fifty-two metres," supplied Angela Singh.

"That's right," said Mr Rigger. "So that means that the correct answer to our question is twenty-four *nautical* miles, which is a bit further than twenty-four miles."

From the back of the class there came a sniggering sound. And then, just loud enough to be heard by Badger but not by Mr Rigger, Geoffrey Shark muttered, "Stupid! Anybody would have known that it was nautical miles and not ordinary miles. Stupid, stupid, stupid!"

Badger bit his lip. He was sure that Shark would not have been able to work it out himself and was in no position to laugh at others.

"Ignore him," whispered Poppy. "Just ignore him."

"I'm glad Badger's not navigating the *Tobermory*," came a loud whisper from Maximilian Flubber.

But this was too much for Poppy, who spun round in her seat and glared in Flubber's direction. "Have you forgotten who saved your life?" she hissed.

Flubber looked away. For a moment he looked ashamed, but then his usual pudding-like expression returned to his face.

Yet Ben, at least, having noticed Flubber's reaction, thought perhaps there was a chance that the unpleasant threesome of Hardtack, Shark and Flubber might not be as united as they would like people to believe. Perhaps sooner or later Flubber or Shark would realise that Hardtack was just dragging them down and they would make a real effort to get away from his influence. But even if they realised this, would they act on it? Could Flubber or Shark ever take that all-important first step of telling Hardtack to his face that they wanted nothing more to do with his tricks and plotting? That would be the real test. Ben was not sure, but, on balance, he thought they would not.

The *Tobermory* made its way down the coast of South America. Now they were off Brazil, the largest country on the continent, and would follow the Brazilian shore until the time came to turn off sharply to the east and head for Australia. The crew knew that once they did that the Roaring Forties would lie ahead. That part of the voyage would be tough, but by now they all had their sea legs and would be able to cope with the deck going violently up and down for days on end. For the time being, though, they had calm waters and a view of beaches and jungle to keep them happy.

Nothing eventful occurred during this section of the journey, except for one thing, which happened to Henry, the Captain's dog. Henry was a popular member of the crew. He had no real duties, although he would sometimes warn smaller boats if they were in the way of the *Tobermory*. In such instances, he would sit up on the prow of the ship and bark loudly as a signal to the other boats that they risked collision if they did not give way to the large sailing ship. Usually, other sailors appreciated his warning and would wave cheerfully to Henry, who would give an encouraging bark in response.

When he was not acting as a look-out in this way, Henry would sometimes take up a position at the rail and look wistfully out to sea. It was no secret what he was doing on these occasions. The story went that

Henry had once dived into the water and brought back a mermaid on board. The mermaid had been none too pleased about this, and after being given a bowl of soup had slithered off the deck, back into the sea. Now, people said, Henry was looking out to sea in the hope of finding another mermaid.

But of course, like so many stories you hear at sea, it simply was not true. Nobody has ever seen a mermaid – not a real one – and there are no photographs to prove that they even exist. So the safest thing to do, when there are no photographs, is to conclude that people are just making things up or passing on a story that someone else has told them.

It was a Saturday morning when there were no lessons. The *Tobermory* was sailing gently along, and although there had to be a few people on watch, helping with the lines or handling the helm, most students were playing chess or cards, or drawing in their sketch books, or writing letters home that would be posted at the next harbour.

Henry was sitting halfway along the main deck, his tail stretched out behind him, enjoying the warmth of the sun on his dark wet nose. He was not thinking of anything in particular – dogs often think of nothing at all – although every now and then he formed a mental picture of his dinner and imagined he could already smell the gravy that would later be ladled into his bowl.

It was while he was day-dreaming in this way that a school of flying fish was swimming past. Flying fish are a very strange sort of fish. Most fish cannot fly, just as most birds cannot swim underwater. Flying fish, though, are equipped with a small set of flippers that act as wings when they launch themselves out of the water. Once they do, their stubby wings flap at high speed, making a whirring sound, just as if they are being powered by a loud clockwork motor. It is a sort of *bbbzzz* sound.

Miss Worsfold had explained all about flying fish during one of her lessons.

"They can't breathe out of water," she said, "so they can't stay in the air too long."

"Then why do they do it?" asked Thomas Seagrape.

"They do it when something's chasing them," Miss Worsfold replied. "When a bigger fish comes after a shoal of flying fish, the one thing they can do that the bigger fish can't is to get out of the water, fly a little way, then drop back into a different bit of water."

Now, as Henry lay on the deck and the students busied themselves with their various hobbies, down below in the water a hungry barracuda – a big fish with very sharp teeth – decided that the small group of flying fish swimming happily nearby would make a perfect midday snack. The flying fish, panicking at the sight of the barracuda, hurled themselves out of the water, flapping their wings as fast as they could.

What they did not notice, though, was the huge bulk of the *Tobermory* immediately in front of them. But it was too late to turn back, so they simply flapped their wings a little harder to gain some extra height and shot over the deck of the great sailing ship and back into the water on the other side.

Henry, who had been dozing, opened his eyes to see a whole cloud of flying fish directly above his nose. No dog could ignore such a challenge, so he went scampering after them, barking furiously and determined to catch some of these insolent creatures. But the fish were too fast for him, and unable to stop himself in time he shot off the edge of the deck, following the flying fish in a perfect arc down into the water.

Henry, of course, was a good swimmer, and there was never any danger of him drowning, but it was still impossible for him to get back on board the *Tobermory* without one of the liberty boats being lowered to pick him up. But before he could even paddle his way back closer to the ship, he was caught by a large wave and carried further away from the *Tobermory* towards the shore.

Other dogs might well have panicked, but Henry, resourceful as ever, managed to clamber on top of a small plank of wood that was also being carried along by the wave, and it was on this improvised surfboard that he sped towards the beach, wagging his tail excitedly.

Down below in the water a hungry barracuda decided that the small group of flying fish would make a perfect midday snack ...

No dog could ignore such a challenge ...

It was a marvellous sight, and there were howls of laughter from the deck of the *Tobermory* ...

It was a marvellous sight, and there were howls of laughter from the deck of the *Tobermory*. Captain Macbeth heard the noise and came up from below to see what was going on. At first he was alarmed to see his dog speeding away in the water, but when he saw Henry surfing, his face broke into a broad smile.

It was a simple matter to stop the ship and launch a small boat, captained by Mr Rigger, to row off and pick up Henry, who by now had been deposited at the edge of the beach, where the waves made a white line of foam.

When he came back on board, he was given a hero's welcome.

"You know," said Mr Rigger, as he watched Henry being dried in one of Matron's large towels, "I thought I'd come across everything there was to see on the oceans, but now … well, Henry is the very first surfing dog I've ever seen!"

Hearing his name mentioned, Henry uttered a bark. A dog's bark can mean many things, but this one seemed clear enough. It said, *Well, there you are, please don't underestimate what I can do!*

CHAPTER 5

Shark takes a shower

The *Tobermory* made it across the Roaring Forties much more quickly than anticipated, even allowing for the time spent rescuing Feathers from his dangerous iceberg. That was not the only ice they saw – they narrowly avoided hitting a large chunk one night when the moon went behind a cloud and it was difficult to see what lay ahead. Poppy and Badger were at the helm when this happened, and they were able to swing the ship sharply to starboard and just miss the ice.

Another incident, potentially just as serious, took place just a few days before they reached Australia. It had to do with water, which is one of the most precious things on any ship when it is at sea. Fresh water, that is – there's any amount of salt water all around you, but you can't drink that. So you have to watch your supplies of fresh water and make sure there's enough to last until you get to the next port.

Like any big ship, the *Tobermory* had large tanks down below in the bilges – the very lowest part of the boat – in which fresh water was stored. Pipes led up from these tanks to the kitchen and then on to the basins and showers in the washrooms. Cook looked after drinking water, decanting it into large containers from which everybody could fill their individual water bottles. He also filled jugs that were placed on the table at mealtimes.

Fresh water was needed in the washrooms because you can't wash in sea water, nor can you brush your teeth in it. Washing in sea water leaves you covered in salt and feeling sticky; only fresh water will make you properly clean.

But you have to be careful. Standing under the shower for a long time might make you feel nice and clean, but it gets through a large volume of water. And if everybody on a ship like the *Tobermory* took long showers, the supplies of fresh water would last no time at all.

Poppy had explained all this to Fee when she first joined the ship. "There's a very important rule when it comes to showers," she explained. "No shower longer than two minutes."

Fee frowned. "Two minutes isn't very long," she said.

"No, it isn't," said Poppy. "It's really just in and out."

"But why?" asked Fee.

"We need to save water," Poppy explained. "There are lots of people on board. If everybody had a long shower – say ten minutes – we'd run out of water way before we reached the next port."

Fee loved long showers, but she understood that these would just not be possible on board. "I'll be careful," she promised.

"Good," said Poppy. "Because if we ran out of water, we wouldn't have anything to drink." She paused before continuing, "There's a famous poem, you know. It's called *The Rime of the Ancient Mariner.* Have you read it?"

Fee shook her head.

"It's about a ship that runs out of water," said Poppy. "It goes like this: *Water, water everywhere, and all the boards did shrink; Water, water everywhere, nor any drop to drink.*"

Fee shivered. "If we ran out of water in the middle of the ocean," she said, "what would happen? Would we die of thirst?"

Poppy shrugged. "If it didn't rain, maybe. You see, if it rains you can collect water in a canvas tarpaulin. You can get quite a bit that way."

Fee was relieved. But then Poppy went on, "*If* it rains … And it doesn't always rain, does it? How much rain have we had in the past few days?" She paused for a few moments before answering her own question. "None. So if we ran out of water now, it wouldn't be good."

Fee was always careful with fresh water after that

– as was everybody, as they heard often enough from the Captain and Matron about the need to conserve supplies. Like everybody else, Fee attended Matron's special classes in how to wash your hair in forty-five seconds (if you were a girl) and thirty seconds (if you were a boy). (The difference, of course, was based on the fact that the girls mostly had longer hair than the boys, and needed more time to wash it.) There were also lessons in how to clean your teeth using less than half a cup of fresh water, and how to wash your clothes in a bucket.

All of the water tanks had gauges on them, and it was part of the duties of the morning watch to check the levels on these gauges, note them down on a piece of paper and report them to the duty officer. One morning, when the *Tobermory* was still several days from Australia, it was the turn of Ben and Badger to check the water levels in the main freshwater tank. Because they had been at sea for so long, the two secondary tanks had been used up and the ship would be dependent on the main tank for the rest of the voyage. The Captain had calculated that there would be enough water to see them through, and nobody was too worried that they might run out.

It was dark down in the bilges, and the only way Ben and Badger could see was to use the powerful flashlight kept near the door for exactly this purpose.

Ben took the flashlight and lit the way down the ladder into the bilges.

"I don't like it down here," he confessed to Badger. "It makes me feel a bit …"

"Scared?" supplied Badger.

"Yes, I suppose so." It is not easy to admit to people that you are scared, but Ben knew that Badger was not the sort of person to laugh at you for not being brave.

"I'm scared too," said Badger

It was dark where they were, and there were all sorts of odd sounds too, which were the creaking and groaning of timbers that are the constant soundtrack of a ship at sea. But there were other sounds too, which were more difficult to identify. There was a buzzing and a whistling, and something that sounded just like footsteps, although that was impossible as they were the only people down there.

Unless the ship is haunted, thought Ben, remembering that he had heard some talk of that, before reassuring himself that people often make up these stories just to frighten each other.

They made their way down to the bottom of the ladder. Now Ben played the beam of light over the short walkway that led to the secondary water tanks – now both empty – to the side of the main water tank. They could already see the gauge illuminated in the darkness, although they could not read the figures.

When they reached the tank, Badger bent down to read the gauge. Ben heard a sharp intake of breath – a gasp.

"The tank's almost empty," whispered Badger. "Only ... only ..." He struggled to make out the markings on the gauge. "I can't quite read it, Ben, but it's hardly registering."

"But that's impossible, Badge," exclaimed Ben. "Take another look."

Badger craned his neck to get a better view. "No," he muttered after a while. "It's almost all gone."

Ben leaned forward to take a look himself. He hoped that Badger had got it wrong, but when he looked at the gauge, it told the same story to him. "Knock on the side of the tank," he said to Badger. "See if it sounds empty."

There is a big difference between the sound that a full tank makes and the sound that an empty one makes. One sounds like a solid block of wood – the other sounds like a drum. This sounded like a drum.

"It's definitely almost empty," said Badger. "Listen to that."

They tried it again. There was no doubt: the main water tank was almost completely dry.

The two boys looked at one another. "What do we do?" asked Ben.

Badger thought for a moment. "We must go and tell the Captain right away," he said. "Because ..." He looked at his watch, and Ben's heart sank. They were up early because they were on watch; everybody else was just about to get up and would be going to the washrooms for a shower. Unless they stopped them, the ship's water supply would be totally exhausted within a couple of minutes.

With only the flashlight to guide them, they scrambled out of the bilges and up the ladder. Then they both ran as fast as they possibly could to the Great Cabin, Captain Macbeth's personal quarters.

The Captain had only just got dressed and was straightening his tie when the two boys knocked loudly at his door. He was surprised to see them and he knew immediately that something was wrong.

"A problem?" he asked.

"Yes," blurted out Badger. "The water … We looked, you see, and we …"

"It was really low," said Ben, who was still panting to catch his breath.

The Captain held up a hand. "Calm down," he said. "Take a deep breath – and then tell me what the trouble is. What water are you talking about?"

"The main tank," said Badger. "We were checking the level this morning …"

"As you should," interjected the Captain. "You're on this watch, aren't you?"

"Yes," said Badger. "So we checked and the gauge was almost at zero. There's hardly any water left."

If it rains you can collect water in a canvas tarpaulin ...

"The tank's almost empty," whispered Badger.

TAP
TAP TAP

"Calm down," said Captain Macbeth. "Take a deep breath – and then tell me what the trouble is ..."

The Captain frowned. "I know the secondary tanks are empty. We've still got the main tank."

Badger shook his head. "No, we haven't, sir. The main tank has hardly any water left, and if people have their showers this morning ..."

The Captain stopped him. "Are you absolutely sure? The main tank?"

Ben confirmed what Badger had said. "Almost empty, Captain," he said. "We checked by knocking on it to see how much was left. If people start to use water ..."

He did not finish. The consequences of that did not have to be spelt out.

If you are the captain of a ship you have to be able to make decisions – and make them quickly. This is what Captain Macbeth now did. Without losing a moment, he rushed to a switch near his desk and pushed it. This was the general alarm, which sounded throughout the whole ship. Everyone had been trained to react to this by making their way up to the main deck immediately, bringing their lifejackets with them. It was a strict rule that the crew came immediately and did not waste time changing or combing their hair or searching for things they might like to take in a lifeboat if they had to abandon ship.

Ben and Badger knew why he had done this. It was the best way of stopping the showers from being used.

But would it work, or was it already too late? If anybody had started to have a shower, or even to use the basins to wash their face, then the last few precious gallons could have drained away by now.

It was quite a sight. Most of the people who came up onto the deck, bleary-eyed from having been woken up so abruptly, were still in their pyjamas. But there were some who had got up early and were already dressed – and one or two of them looked as if they had already had a shower.

"Pay attention!" shouted the Captain once the last of the stragglers had appeared. "We are facing a serious water crisis – nobody is to use the showers or the basins until further notice. Drinking water will be rationed by Cook. The toilets may be used as normal – they flush with sea water."

It was clear to everybody that the Captain was angry. After he had finished speaking, he turned to speak to Mr Rigger. Poppy, who was standing nearby, heard every word.

"How on earth did this happen, Mr Rigger?" the Captain asked. "According to my calculations we had plenty of water to see us through – and now this. If there's a leak, then I want to know why it wasn't spotted earlier."

"I'll do what I can to find out," Mr Rigger replied.

The Captain nodded, but he was still obviously concerned. "This is a very serious situation, you know," he muttered to Mr Rigger. "More serious than the students might realise."

Mr Rigger glanced over his shoulder. "We don't want them to panic," he said quietly.

"No," agreed the Captain. "We'll keep an appearance of normality as much as possible, but I must say I'm very, very worried."

After the Captain had finished his announcement, there was a buzz of excited chatter. A water crisis? Why was there a water crisis when everything had seemed to be fine the day before? Nobody had said anything then about the tank running dry. Ben and Badger went to join their friends, who were eager to find out what had happened.

"Are you absolutely sure you were reading the right gauge?" asked Poppy.

"Absolutely sure," confirmed Badger. "We both looked, didn't we, Ben? Just to be certain."

Ben nodded. "We also knocked on the tank to see if it sounded empty – and it did. It was just like a great big drum."

"I heard the Captain talking to Mr Rigger," said Poppy. "He said we're in serious trouble. And he must be right: we're miles from Australia and the nearest fresh water."

Tanya shook her head sadly. "What will happen when Cook's supply of drinking water is used up? What then?"

Poppy shrugged. "I don't know. And how long is that going to last, anyway? A day at the most, I think."

Breakfast was a sombre affair. Although everybody was trying to put a brave face on it, they all knew just how serious the situation was. Cook did his best to appear cheerful, but it was clear that he was worried. He usually chatted in a friendly way with people when they came to collect their food, but that morning he was tight-lipped.

"Are we going to be all right, Cook?" asked Badger as he waited for Cook to put his egg and sausage onto his plate.

Cook liked Badger and would not normally have snapped at him. But that morning his reply was short and unfriendly. "What do you think?" he said angrily. "Do you expect me to produce water from nowhere? Don't ask stupid questions."

Badger was taken aback. "Sorry, Cook," he stuttered. "I was just asking …"

Cook immediately regretted his bad temper. "No, I'm the one who should be saying sorry, young Badger," he said. "It's just that … well, I don't really know what to do. I'm down to a few pints of water, and when I turned on the tap nothing came out – just a hissing sound. I'm afraid I'm getting really worried, and that made me bite your head off. I'm sorry about that."

Badger told him that it did not matter. "I'm sure

the Captain will find a solution," he said. He was not sure of that, of course, but he wanted to say something to cheer Cook up, and he thought this would be better than saying nothing.

Badger returned to his table. "What did Cook say?" asked Poppy. "Did he have any ideas?"

Badger shook his head. "Nothing much," he replied. "I think he's every bit as worried as the rest of us."

They looked at one another, but nobody said anything. And what was there to say? Talking can make you thirsty, and so it was probably best to say nothing at all.

Then suddenly a boy from another table, Bartholomew Fitzhardy, came up and whispered into Badger's ear. He was popular and was also one of the most skilful sailors in the school. He was not the sort to exaggerate or make up stories.

"I want to tell you something," said Bartholomew.

"Well, I'm listening," said Badger.

Bartholomew looked over his shoulder. "Not in here. Outside – on deck."

Badger looked puzzled, but he could tell that it was important. "Can Ben come?" he asked. "He knows how to keep a secret."

Bartholomew hesitated for a moment, but then he nodded. "All right. I'll go out first – you and Ben wait a few minutes and then come. I'll be on the port side – near the lifebelt locker."

Badger leaned over towards Ben and told him that they would need to go up on deck. Ben nodded; he had guessed that Bartholomew wanted to talk to Badger in private and he was glad that he had been invited too.

A few minutes later they left their table in the mess hall and made their way out on deck. Bartholomew was waiting for them exactly where he said he would be.

"What's up?" asked Badger.

Bartholomew spoke quietly. There was nobody else around, but he still seemed to be anxious about what he was about to say.

"Last night," he said. "I took a shower really late, just before lights out. It was a quick shower and I had dried off and changed into my pyjamas. I turned off the lights in the washroom because I guessed that nobody else would be coming in after me. But as I came out of the door, I bumped into Geoffrey Shark. He had his towel and sponge bag with him, so I realised he was going to have a shower." He paused. "In fact, I *knew* that he was going to have a shower because he said to me, 'I hope you've left me some hot water, Fitzhardy.' You know how rudely those three talk. It was like that."

Badger waited for Bartholomew to continue.

"Well," Bartholomew went on, "when I got back to my cabin I realised I had left my sponge bag in the washroom, so I went back and when I reached the washroom door I met Shark. He had finished his shower and was going back to his cabin. He was carrying my sponge bag, and he said to me, 'You left this behind, Fitzhardy – I was going to bring it to you.' I thanked him and turned to go back to my cabin. As I did so, though, I heard the shower running inside. I thought somebody else had come to take a shower after Shark."

He paused, lowering is voice. "But there can't have been anyone there – because this morning I realised that Shark had turned the lights out. In fact I saw him do it. I didn't really think anything about it at the time, but now I realise Shark must have left the shower running *all night.*"

Ben drew in his breath. "All night!" he whispered.

"Yes," said Bartholomew. "And that must be why we've got no water. Shark let it all run down the drain."

Badger winced. "I suppose he didn't mean to."

"No," said Bartholomew. "He can't have meant to, but it is his fault, isn't it? It's his fault that we have no water left."

Ben looked at Badger. "What are we going to do?" he asked.

Badger thought for a moment. "I want to talk to Poppy and the others. In the meantime, Barty, I think we should keep quiet about this."

Bartholomew nodded. "I just felt I had to tell you," he said. "But I won't tell anybody else."

"Good," said Badger. "Keep it that way for the time being."

CHAPTER 6

Stealing water

That morning, Poppy and Fee were on helm duty for a half-watch, with Mr Rigger as Duty Officer. The winds had become much lighter as they neared Australia, and the seas were calm, so there was not much to do but to follow the course for land. It was, in fact, quite a dull task for them, and would have been even duller had they not had rather a lot to think about. And those thoughts were all about water.

If you've ever been really thirsty and not been able to fill yourself a glass of water, then you will know that the last thing you should do is to think about water. That just makes it worse. But that morning, as the *Tobermory* made its way towards Australia with almost completely dry tanks, water was the only thing on everybody's mind.

And it was not just the members of the crew who were affected by the water shortage. Henry was particularly unhappy. His drinking bowl, normally filled to the brim, now held only a few drops, and he sat panting, wondering why it was that his bowl had so suddenly dried up.

There was little fresh water for Feathers the penguin too. "I bet he wishes he were back on his iceberg," said Fee, before remembering one of Miss Worsfold's lessons on marine life about how penguins can also drink salt water. So Feathers was quite happy to dive into the sea from the deck of the *Tobermory* and drink as much as he wanted during his daily swim.

Mr Rigger was normally one of the most cheerful of the teachers, but now Poppy and Fee did not see so much as a trace of a smile on his lips. Even his moustache, normally such a fine feature of his appearance, was drooping badly.

Poppy decided to ask him directly what would happen. "How bad are things, Mr Rigger?" she enquired.

Mr Rigger did not answer for a while, and Poppy wondered whether he had heard her question. But then he spoke, in a voice that sounded tired and low. "Pretty bad, Poppy. By my reckoning, we're still several days from the closest port. We'll have to turn on the engines to give us a bit of extra speed, but even then I'm not sure …"

He did not finish his sentence, but sighed in a way that indicated that he had nothing further to say – or at least nothing that would make her feel any better.

"But what about drinking water?" asked Fee.

Mr Rigger shrugged. "Cook has put what we have left into bottles," he said. "There'll be one bottle between three people."

"One bottle between three!" exclaimed Poppy as she worked out how little that would amount to. It would be a small sip in the morning and one at night – at the most – if the bottle were to last more than a couple of days.

Mr Rigger nodded miserably. "It's not much," he said. "But what choice do we have?"

Poppy looked up at the sky. "If it rains, we'll be all right," she said.

Mr Rigger tried to look cheerful. "Yes," he said. "You're right, Poppy. And I'm sure it'll rain. I'm sure of that."

They knew, though, that Mr Rigger was just doing his best to make them feel better. That was his job, after all – to get the best out of the crew, and nobody is at his or her best if they are feeling down in the dumps.

Then Mr Rigger asked a question. Of all the questions he could ask, this was probably the most awkward one – but he was not to know that.

"I wonder why we ran out of water," he began. "What could it have been?"

He addressed the question to both of them, and they both looked away – Fee looking to port, and

Poppy looking to starboard. And Mr Rigger noticed this. He was an observant man – as all sailors tend to be – and he could tell that his question had unsettled them.

"It could have been anything," said Poppy. "It could have been a leak."

It was not a lie – Poppy would never want to tell a lie – but it was not a completely truthful answer either.

Mr Rigger was looking at her intently, and Poppy felt herself blushing.

"Do you know something about it, Poppy?" Mr Rigger asked. "You should tell me if you do."

Poppy glanced at Fee, who looked down at the deck in confusion. Feeling very uncomfortable, Poppy nodded her head. "I'm not sure if I know in the sense of being one-hundred-per-cent sure, but …"

"But we sort-of know," interjected Fee.

They both felt uneasy because, as in any school, there was an understanding on the *Tobermory* that you did not tell tales, though everybody knew that there were times when you had to tell the teachers if somebody was doing something dangerous, for example, or somebody was bullying somebody else. But it was not always easy to do this. It could make you unpopular. It was hard.

"You 'sort-of know'?" said Mr Rigger. "Well, in my mind you either know something or you don't. There can't be any 'sort-of knowing'."

Poppy thought about this before she answered. "We've been told something," she said at last. "We've been told that …" She hesitated. "We've been told that somebody left a shower running all night."

Mr Rigger looked grave. "I see," he said. "Well, that would certainly drain the tank, I suppose."

"Yes," said Poppy. "But he probably didn't mean it."

Mr Rigger considered this. "No," he said. "I suppose he didn't. Still, it was extreme carelessness."

"Yes," said Fee. "It's just the sort of thing that Shark …"

She stopped herself, putting a hand to her mouth as if to catch the words. But they were already out, and the one thing you can never do with words is put them back in your mouth.

"Shark!?" exclaimed Mr Rigger.

Neither girl spoke, and that was enough to confirm it.

"That boy," muttered Mr Rigger, shaking his head. "I should have realised." He was going to say something more, but he stopped himself. As a rule, teachers did not discuss students with other students, but every so often something came out to show what they were thinking.

"What are you going to do?" asked Poppy.

"This is a difficult situation, you know," he said. "Shark's carelessness has put all our lives in danger. That's not a small thing. And the Captain will have to be told about it."

Poppy looked worried. "But if Shark thinks we told you about it ... what then?"

"What Shark thinks is neither here nor there," said Mr Rigger. "If he was careless, then he will have to be confronted about it and suffer the consequences. And he'll certainly be told to be more careful in future."

Mr Rigger saw how uncomfortable Poppy looked. He tried to reassure her. "I don't want you to worry about any of this," he said. "I won't reveal how I found out about it."

Poppy said nothing, but she was secretly pleased.

"I've an idea," Mr Rigger continued. "Perhaps we should give Shark the chance to own up. He'll still be punished, perhaps not so severely, but he could at least to say sorry for his carelessness."

"He won't do that," said Poppy. "He's not like that."

"Shall we see?" said Mr Rigger. "Not everybody is completely bad, you know."

"They are," said Fee, referring to the unfriendly trio of Hardtack, Shark and Flubber.

Mr Rigger shook his head. "No, even him. Even Hardtack will have some good in him." He paused. "I'm going to have a word with Shark. I'm going to ask him if it has occurred to him that he might have left the shower running. And then I'll see what he says."

"He'll lie," said Poppy. "He always does."

"We'll see," said Mr Rigger.

As the day wore on, the *Tobermory* crew began to feel the impact of the water rationing. Having been issued with their precious bottles of water, the students kept a close eye on the level, making sure that nobody had more than his or her fair share. Ben and Badger were sharing with Thomas Seagrape, and each of them, of course, was very careful not to take more than a small sip when the bottle was handed round. But there were arguments elsewhere. Angela Singh, who was sharing with a set of twins known for their selfishness, Molly and Lolly, complained that they had taken large gulps rather than sips and had finished almost half the bottle in one go. And poor Bartholomew Fitzhardy spilled half of his bottle when he put it down without checking that the cap was screwed on properly. That did not go down well with the people he was sharing with, who said that the water that had been spilled would be treated as his share and therefore he was not entitled to any further sips. Ben felt sorry for Bartholomew and agreed with Badger and Thomas that he could have some of their water instead.

By and large, though, everybody behaved well in the emergency except for … well, it was inevitable that if there was going to be any bad behaviour William Edward Hardtack and his gang would be mixed up in it somewhere. And what they did was so shocking that people found it hard to believe.

Miss Worsfold, who taught classes on geography and marine life, was of course interested in all sorts of fish and had a large fish tank in her cabin. In this she kept a number of small, highly colourful tropical fish. People were allowed to visit these fish from time to time, and just about the whole school had been introduced to them and had been allowed to give them small helpings of fish food.

When she returned to her cabin later that afternoon, Miss Worsfold saw to her surprise that the tank was only half full: somebody had taken water from it. Fortunately, her fish were still alive, but were now obliged to swim backwards and forwards in a much smaller amount of water. They were not at all happy about this.

Word soon got around the ship as to what had happened.

"Who on earth would do something like that?" asked Fee. "Imagine stealing water from fish!"

Nobody had been seen going into the staff cabins, so anyone who had suspicions about who was responsible kept them quiet. But it was not long before the mystery was solved – in a quite unexpected manner.

It was at dinner. By then everybody was feeling extremely thirsty. Thankfully, a little more water had been produced by melting some ice from the ship's large freezers, but it was only enough to give every-body a small glassful. Still, that managed to relieve the worst symptoms of thirst and it resulted in a more cheerful atmosphere at dinner. Clouds had been spotted on the horizon, and that too helped raise the mood.

"They look like rain clouds," Mr Rigger observed.

If it rained, then the tanks would soon be filled with fresh water.

But at dinner that night it was not the possibility of rain that was the subject of conversation. Rather, it was about what happened to Hardtack and his friends shortly after the meal was served. They had just taken their seats when Hardtack suddenly gave a loud groan and clutched his stomach. No sooner had he done this than Maximilian Flubber emitted a similar groan, to be followed seconds later by Geoffrey Shark.

"Look at Hardtack," whispered Poppy to Fee. "I'd say that he has a rather sore stomach."

"And his pals too," said Fee. "Look – Flubber's turned green."

By now the whole mess hall was riveted by what was happening at Hardtack's table, so everybody saw it when he rose to his feet, followed closely by Flubber and Shark, and ran, half-stumbling, towards the door.

It was Poppy who first guessed what had happened. "That's it!" she exclaimed. "They must have

drunk the water from Miss Worsfold's fish tank. And it would have been full of fish food."

Badger's mouth dropped open in astonishment. "Of course," he said. "Of course that's what must have happened. You know what fish eat? Ants' eggs. That stuff they give fish is actually ants' eggs."

"So when they drank the poor fishes' water," Fee joined in, "they also got a mouthful of ants' eggs. No wonder they don't feel well."

It was hard not to laugh. Nobody would have wished serious illness on Hardtack and his friends, but a little discomfort and nausea – well, that was another matter.

Mr Rigger had seen what was happening and had followed the three boys to check that they were all right. When he came back a few minutes later, Poppy asked him whether he thought the sudden departure of Hardtack and his friends had anything to do with Matron's half-emptied fish tank. He did not answer directly, but Poppy could tell that her guess was correct.

"Put it this way," said Mr Rigger, "whoever drank that water will not do anything quite so stupid again – at least, not in a hurry!"

The clouds did bring rain that night. As the wind rose, sheets of rain swept across the waves and foaming water. And as it fell, it was collected in the tarpaulin spread out on the deck of the *Tobermory* and transferred by pipes down to the tanks below. These were soon full – all three of them – giving the ship more than enough fresh water to reach Australia.

"The emergency's over," announced the Captain the next morning. "You may all have showers, wash your hands and fill your water bottles – all those things are now allowed."

Up on deck, Mr Rigger called Poppy over to have a word with her. "Now that the emergency's over," he said, "I thought I might tell you that I spoke to Geoffrey Shark this morning. I'm happy to say he was very apologetic about what he did. He's going to the Captain of his own accord to apologise."

Poppy could not conceal her surprise. "I never thought he would," she said.

"Well, there you are," said Mr Rigger. "Sometimes people behave better than we think they will."

Later that morning, Poppy told Badger what Mr Rigger had said about Shark. "I think he may have learned a lesson," she said. "And Flubber and Hardtack as well."

"I hope so," said Badger. "But you never know with people like that. You may think that they've become better, and then all of a sudden and with no warning they do something nasty."

Poppy thought about this. She suspected that Badger was right, but she was unwilling to give up entirely on Hardtack, Shark and Flubber. There was still plenty of time for them to show another side to their character – and perhaps Australia would bring that out. Time would tell.

CHAPTER 7

Boomerang

They arrived in Sydney early in the morning. The *Tobermory* had been sailing all night and Poppy and Fee were on the watch ending just before sunrise. They knew they were close to land and that the bank of fog off their port bow was concealing Sydney, with its famous Harbour Bridge and Opera House. They both wanted to stay on deck to see these when the fog lifted, but there was a rule that those who had been on the last watch of the night had to go to their cabins to rest. So they went down below, climbed into their bunks and quickly fell asleep, rocked by the motion of the ship as it completed the last few miles of their journey.

By the time the two girls awoke, the *Tobermory* had sailed past the protective arms of land at the entrance to Sydney Harbour. Without wasting any time, they joined the rest of the crew on deck, watching as the famous skyline revealed itself to them. Poppy was particularly excited, as Australia was her home and she knew that her parents had travelled from Alice

Springs to be there to welcome them.

"There's the bridge!" she called out excitedly. "I've climbed that, you know."

Fee gazed at the famous bridge, a high arc of steel joining the two sides of the harbour. From a distance, it looked like a great steel rainbow.

"You went up *there*?" she asked, imagining what it must be like at the top of the great structure.

"It's quite safe," said Poppy. "They hook you to a wire so that you can't fall."

By now they were moving through the water very slowly, the sails having been dropped and the ship's engines set to low power. A great sailing ship like the *Tobermory* always attracts attention, and smaller boats were coming out to meet her, circling her playfully, their crews waving a welcome. Several boats sounded their horns in salute, and the *Tobermory* replied with hers – a long, low sound that echoed over the water.

When they reached their berth, the Captain ordered the anchor to be lowered. With a loud clanking sound, followed by a splash, the anchor disappeared into the sea, the heavy links of its chain rattling behind it. Once it had reached the sea-bed, more chain was let out to make sure that the ship would not tug itself free. With the anchor set, the Captain gave the order to turn off the engines. Suddenly there was silence, and it was in this silence, with the high, sun-filled Australian sky above them, that everyone stood on deck and gazed at the scene before them. Fee felt as if she had to pinch herself – *I'm really here,* she thought. *I'm really here in Sydney.*

Most people were keen to go ashore straight away, but there were formalities to be completed first. The Captain had to notify the authorities of exactly who was on board and who would be going ashore, and only once he had done this would it be possible for the liberty boats to ferry groups of students to dry land. But that was soon sorted out, and the first of the boats was able to make the short journey to the nearby quay.

Poppy and Fee were in the first boat, along with Angela, Ben and Thomas. Poppy could hardly contain her excitement, and when she saw her parents waiting on the quay she almost upset the boat with her waving, such was her enthusiasm.

"Careful!" shouted Mr Rigger. "You'll have us all in the water." But he smiled as he shouted the warning, realising how excited she must be.

Once ashore and united with her parents, Poppy introduced her friends. Then they all made their way to a café for lunch. Over the meal, Poppy gave her mother and father a full account of everything that had happened on the voyage – including the rescue of Feathers, Henry's experience of surfing and the water shortage.

Poppy's father frowned as she told him of the stupidity and selfishness of Hardtack and his friends.

"I know people like that," he said. "You don't want them around you in the Outback, where we all have to rely on one another."

"Do you think they'll ever change?" asked Poppy's mother. She turned to her husband. "Remember that fellow who was in that group that got lost. He made off with the food and water, thinking he'd get back to town by himself."

"He left them out in the bush?" asked Poppy incredulously.

"Yes," said her mother. "He went off by himself. He didn't care about the others."

"And what happened?" asked Badger.

Poppy's mother paused for a moment. "What happened? Well, he tripped over a rock and broke his ankle. He dragged himself to the shade of a tree and waited. There was nothing else he could do."

"But you can't last long out there," interjected Poppy. "It's far too hot."

"That's right," said her mother. "Meanwhile, the others wandered around, becoming more and more lost, until one of them worked out the way back. And they were well on their way home when they came across the fellow who'd run off with the supplies. He was still lying under his tree, looking pretty far gone. But they picked him up and carried him home to town. He was too weak to walk, but they saved his life."

"He was lucky," observed Ben. "He thought he'd save himself, but ended up being saved by the people he'd left behind."

"That's true," said Poppy's father. "And that's worth remembering, I think. You may think you're all right on your own, but you never know when you're going to need other people."

After they finished their lunch, Poppy went off with her parents for some private time while the others explored the streets around the harbour. There were all sorts of shops, and having had nothing to spend their pocket money on for weeks, there was much to tempt them. Ben and Badger bought wide-brimmed Australian bush-hats; Fee treated herself to a pair of Outback boots; and Angela and Thomas bought themselves boomerangs. Then, once back at the quay, they signalled to Mr Rigger, who was standing on the deck of the *Tobermory*, admiring the view. He returned their signal and rowed across the harbour to collect them.

"I see you've bought boomerangs," he said to Thomas and Angela as they climbed into the rowing boat. "Do you know how to throw them?"

Both shook their heads. Thomas had seen a film of somebody throwing one, though, and he thought it looked quite easy. Angela had been reading the small instruction leaflet that came with her boomerang. This made it look simple, but instruction leaflets often do that – and she was not confident.

Mr Rigger laughed. "I've thrown a boomerang before," he said. "Would you like me to show you?"

Both Angela and Thomas agreed. Mr Rigger was good at showing you how to do things, and they had confidence in him.

Once back on the *Tobermory*, they gathered around Mr Rigger for the demonstration. "You hold it like this," said Mr Rigger, grasping the end of Angela's boomerang in his right hand. "Then you draw your arm back – like this. And then …" They watched with bated breath as he hurled the boomerang into the air. Angela gasped as she watched it fly at high speed over the water. Further and further it went, showing no sign of coming back. She was sure that sooner or later it would lose momentum, fall into the sea and be lost. But then the boomerang suddenly started to turn to the left.

"Look!" said Thomas. "It's coming back."

And so it was. Almost as if being controlled by some hidden force, the boomerang began to return towards the *Tobermory*. As if by magic, it swooped up to and over the deck, still wobbling in its curious way, but more slowly. Angela was worried that it would not stop – that it would spin across the deck and disappear over the other side, but she had not reckoned for Henry. The Captain's dog had been sitting near the main mast, enjoying the sunshine, when he suddenly

They arrived in Sydney early in the morning . . .

"There's the bridge!" Poppy called out excitedly. "I've climbed that, you know."

Henry leapt up and with flawless judgement caught the boomerang in his jaws.

saw a strange flying object coming towards him. Unable to resist the temptation, Henry leapt up, launched himself into the air and with flawless judgement caught the boomerang in his jaws.

This feat was greeted by a great cheer from all who witnessed it.

"Well done, Henry!" shouted Angela, relieved that her trophy had not been lost forever.

Henry wagged his tail and made his way over to Mr Rigger and dropped the boomerang at his feet. Rewarded with a pat on the head and a promise of an extra dog biscuit that evening, Henry trotted back to his place near the mast.

"You see," said Mr Rigger, with a wink. "Easy, isn't it?"

Later that day the entire ship's company gathered on deck to say goodbye to Feathers. Although there were many who wanted the penguin to stay – not least Feathers himself, who had become quite comfortable on board – the Captain had decided that it would be much kinder to the bird to arrange a new home for him with other penguins. Fortunately, the large zoo on the other side of the bay was home to a colony of penguins, and the director had been only too willing to give Feathers a new home.

"Penguins are sociable creatures," the director explained when he came on board the *Tobermory* with two assistants and a portable penguin carrier. "They're never really happy on their own. They need the company of other penguins."

Everybody could understand that, so when they said goodbye to Feathers, although they felt sad, nobody felt that sending him to the zoo was the wrong thing to do.

"I'll send you photographs," said the director. "And we'll make sure that there's a notice outside the enclosure saying that he was rescued by the crew of the *Tobermory*."

From inside his carrier, Feathers could be seen peeping out at his friends. Henry came up and gave the bars of the carrier a lick; this was his way of showing he was sorry his new friend was going. But he, too, appeared to understand that going to the zoo was the best thing for Feathers and did not make a fuss when the carrier was lowered over the side into the zoo's waiting launch.

It was now time for a briefing by the Captain. Standing on the quarter-deck so that everybody could see him, Captain Macbeth addressed the school.

"Members of the ship's company," he began. "We have had an exciting voyage, but now we are here in Australia and about to begin the next stage of our adventure. Tomorrow morning, at first light, we shall sail out of Sydney Harbour and begin our journey up the coast. Our destination is the Great Barrier Reef, where we will spend a day or two before going into harbour at a town called Cairns.

"Cairns is where the Tall Ships race begins, and once that happens I want every single one of you to concentrate on the business in hand – which will be the race. For two weeks there will be less school work, as you will all be busy with the demanding task of trimming our sails and ensuring that the *Tobermory* sails as fast as she possibly can.

"You might be wondering what lies ahead," the Captain continued. "I'd like to be able to say to you that it will all be easy, but the one thing a captain must never do is mislead his crew. So I shall tell you that it's going to be really tough. It's going to be a hard task, and we're up against some stiff competition. The other crews will fight this race right to the end.

"And there's something else. At times it will be dangerous. There are things you are going to have to be extremely careful about. There are great big crocodiles, the saltwater crocodile, or 'salty' as it's called. They live as happily in fresh water as in the sea. Look out for these and remember they are among the most dangerous creatures in the world. Then there are jellyfish that can give you a very nasty sting. And there are sea-snakes that are among the most poisonous snakes in the world. So I want you all to take great care – not just when you think there might be danger about, but every single minute of the day."

The Captain paused, to let his words sink in. And they did. At the mention of crocodiles there was a buzz of anxious conversation as people sought reassurance from their friends and deck prefects.

But not everybody took the warning seriously. "Crocodiles!" sneered William Edward Hardtack. "I'm not sacred of them. They're just overgrown lizards."

"That's right," added Geoffrey Shark. "If I see a crocodile up there, I'm going to make it into a handbag for my mum!"

"Ha!" said Maximilian Flubber, not to be outdone. "I'd like to meet the croc that would dare take me on."

Hearing these remarks, Badger shook his head in amazement. How could anybody be so stupid as to talk like that about such dangerous creatures? He had read all about these Australian crocodiles, and he knew what a threat they could be. Only a few months ago the newspapers had carried the story of a teenager who had been eaten by a saltwater crocodile when he had been fooling around on the banks of a river. Everyone knew that there had been crocodiles about, but the boy had seemed to think they would not be interested in him. But he had been as wrong as he possibly could be. Crocodiles are *very* interested in people and like to get *really* close to them. In fact, crocodiles like people so much that they like to have them *inside* them . . . in their stomachs.

Poppy had come back from her outing with her parents in time to hear the Captain's talk. She told her friends that everything the Captain said was true, and that if Flubber thought he knew better, he was in for a nasty surprise.

"Australia's a great place," she said to Fee. "Some people get the wrong idea and think it's full of things that will bite or eat you given half a chance. That's not really true, but there are times when you have to be careful." She paused. "Most creatures, you know, will get out of your way if they possibly can."

Fee thought about this. She was comfortable enough with most animals, but she was not too keen on spiders. The trouble with them, of course, is that they are so small that most of the time you do not even see them. Of course there are also some rather big spiders – and Australia has plenty of those – but you might not notice them unless they get very close. And hadn't she read somewhere about a girl who had discovered a nest of spiders in her hair?

Tanya was more frightened of snakes. She asked Poppy whether she had ever been really close to a snake – and what was it like?

"Oh, we see snakes all the time in the Outback," said Poppy. "There's a snake called the eastern brown snake – you see lots of them. Sometimes they even come into our house."

Tanya shuddered. "Inside the house?" she asked in

a shocked tone. "Actually inside?"

Poppy smiled. "It's not that bad," she said. "They don't come in and sit at the table and try to eat your breakfast, or anything like that."

Tanya did not think this funny. Nothing about snakes was funny in her view.

"They just slide around on the floor," Poppy continued. "They like to curl up in cool places – under the bath-tub, behind the cupboard – that sort of thing. You usually see them in good time."

"And then?" asked Tanya, her jaw quivering.

"And then my dad comes and takes them outside. He uses a special pole with a hook at the end. He picks them up and puts them down on the grass."

"And if they bite you?" asked Tanya.

"You try not to let them," said Poppy calmly. "But if one of those brown snakes bites you, you're in trouble. We have an antidote to their poison in the fridge, but you can get pretty sick all the same. You can die, if you're unlucky."

"I'd die of fright," said Tanya. "Just seeing a snake would be enough."

Poppy thought of something. "If you think brown snakes are dangerous, you should see the western taipan."

Tanya did *not* want to see a western taipan – and would have preferred not to talk about them, but Fee was interested.

"That's even more poisonous?" she asked.

Poppy nodded. "If one of them bites you, you've got no chance," she said. "But fortunately they're very rare. You only find them in a very small part of Australia, close to the middle, where New South Wales, South Australia and Queensland meet."

Tanya's hand shot to her mouth. "But isn't Queensland where we're going?"

"Not the part they live in," Poppy reassured her.

Fee had had enough of snake talk by now. "Let's talk about nicer animals," she said. And then she added, "Like the duck-billed platypus …"

Poppy smiled. "All right, but there's one thing I need to tell you: the platypus has a poisonous spike on its tail. They look nice and cuddly, but I wouldn't get too close to them."

Tanya groaned. "I'm staying on board ship," she said.

"Fair enough," said Poppy. "But be extra careful not to fall in the water."

Tanya waited for an explanation.

"Great white sharks," said Poppy simply.

CHAPTER 8

The giant clam

It took them almost a week to sail up the coast from Sydney to the Great Barrier Reef. It would have taken them even longer had the winds not been so favourable, but with a strong breeze on their beam they were able to make better progress than the Captain had imagined. They sailed as quickly at night as they did during the day, checking their position by the stars as they travelled and then plotting their course on paper in the chart room. The skies were clear from dusk onwards – great sweeps of dark velvet with the constellations scattered about them like silver dust.

Mr Rigger was the expert on the stars, pointing out the Southern Cross and other constellations that could tell you exactly where you were if you had the right tables to work with. "Don't rely on your GPS," he warned one day in class. "Things can go wrong."

Everyone on board knew this was true. "Anything can happen at sea," was one of Mr Rigger's favourite sayings – and, like a number of his favourite sayings, it was absolutely true.

But now Mr Rigger asked a question. "And just what can go wrong with your GPS?" he asked.

"The battery can go flat," said Poppy. "Without any power, you can't pick up the signal from the satellites."

Mr Rigger nodded. "Good answer," he said. "We rely on batteries, don't we? And then, when they go flat, we don't know what to do, do we?"

Hardtack put up his hand. Badger turned to watch him. Hardtack could usually be relied upon to come up with some smart remark.

"Yes, Hardtack?" said Mr Rigger.

"We can recharge them," said Hardtack, with a smile. "You plug them in and recharge them. Simple."

Flubber and Shark both giggled, but were silenced by a look from Mr Rigger.

"I suppose you think that's funny, Hardtack," Mr Rigger said.

Hardtack pretended to look surprised. "No, sir," he said. "I mean it seriously. Don't you recharge after your battery runs flat? I do that with my phone, sir – not that you allow us to use our phones on board."

There were sounds of agreement from one or two people. Not everybody liked having their phones taken away from them at the start of a voyage, although some students were quite happy to be out of touch with the world when at sea.

Hardtack smirked as he continued. "I recharge, sir. Then things work. It's like magic, sir – but it's really just electricity."

Again Flubber and Shark giggled. Then Shark said, "Hardtack's right, Mr Rigger. If your battery runs flat, you plug in and recharge." He paused. "I could show you, if you like, sir."

Mr Rigger very rarely lost his temper, but it was clear that he was now being pushed to the limit. "If you think this is so amusing, Hardtack, perhaps you might care to go and tell the Captain all about it."

This worked, and Hardtack said nothing more. Talking back to Mr Rigger was one thing; showing disrespect to the Captain was quite another.

"So," continued Mr Rigger, now that Hardtack had been silenced, "the reason why you wouldn't be able to take Hardtack's advice would be that …"

Fee put up her hand. "There's no electricity when you're a hundred miles from anywhere."

"Exactly," said Mr Rigger. "And apart from having a flat battery, your GPS might be broken …"

"Or have been dropped into the water," suggested Ben.

"Yes," said Mr Rigger. "And that happens, you know. You'd be surprised to know how many people drop important things. It happens all the time." He paused. "So it's useful to have other means of knowing where you are."

Later, Badger was to remember this conversation and realise that every word that Mr Rigger said was utterly true. Australia is a big place, and there are plenty of opportunities for getting lost there.

Poppy and Fee were both on watch when the first signs of the Great Barrier Reef appeared on the horizon. To begin with, Poppy thought that her eyes might be playing tricks on her, but when Fee called out she knew she had not been mistaken.

"Something up ahead," shouted Fee, who had gone to stand by the rail on the starboard side of the ship while Poppy stayed on duty at the wheel. "Can you see it?"

Poppy shouted out that she thought she could. And at the same time, from up in the crow's nest, came Badger's voice at full volume. "Reef ahead!" he shouted. "Fifteen degrees off the starboard bow."

Mr Rigger now appeared from down below, followed a few moments later by the Captain himself.

"Reef ahead off the starboard bow, Captain," reported Poppy. "About five nautical miles away."

Captain Macbeth had his telescope with him, and he now extended it to its full length and looked in the direction of the reef. "That's it, sure enough," he said. "Well navigated, everybody."

Orders were given to reduce the amount of sail. Almost immediately, the great ship responded and slowed down in the water like a runner who has reached the end of a long race.

The Captain took the helm from Poppy, who stood down and was congratulated on her fine steering. Then he and Mr Rigger discussed their best approach and gave orders to the new watch coming on duty. More canvas was taken down and the restraining ropes on some of the sails slackened. Now the ship was barely travelling at walking pace, as its bow pointed directly at the waves breaking over the distant coral.

They had to be careful. A reef will cut straight through the hull of even the strongest ship, and once that happens the ship is usually doomed. What they had to do was to get as close as they could without running aground on any of the coral outcrops. Then, once they had anchored, they would be able to approach the reef itself in one of the liberty boats – a much safer way of moving among the little outcrops of coral that made up the barrier.

Captain Macbeth found just the right spot to anchor. As he gave the command for the anchor to be lowered, a great clanking of chains was followed by a great splash as the anchor hit the water. Once enough chain had been laid, the noise stopped, although the boat was still being blown by the wind. The chain, now lying on the shallow sea floor down below, was pulled tight by the movement of the boat as the anchor settled. With a shudder, the *Tobermory* came to a halt, straining against the anchor and its chain, but not moving so much as an inch backwards or forwards.

The Captain called the entire ship's company on deck.

"We're going to spend the rest of the day here," he announced. "Everybody will have the chance to go snorkelling, and those of you who have passed your basic diving certificate can do scuba diving with Miss Worsfold."

Badger turned to Ben and gave him a high five. "That's us," he said proudly.

"And me," said Poppy, her voice full of excitement.

They were some of the few students who had taken Mr Rigger's introductory course when the *Tobermory* had recently been in the Caribbean. This had involved studying the rules of diving with an oxygen cylinder, as well as some short practice dives. There had been few places in the course, as the diving equipment on the *Tobermory* was limited, and those who had been chosen considered themselves lucky. Now there would be a chance to use those skills again, this time in one of the most exciting places of all to dive – a living coral reef with all that went with it: fish, turtles, and … sharks.

Miss Worsfold called the divers to a meeting. There were ten of them altogether – eleven counting herself. The group included not only Poppy, Ben and

Amanda Birtwhistle

Badger, but also Bartholomew Fitzhardy and Amanda Birtwhistle, who was known for being an expert navigator. Thomas Seagrape was also a member of the group. Thomas had a lot of experience of diving at home in the Caribbean and could hold his breath underwater for longer than anybody else on board.

Miss Worsfold went over the safety rules.

"Never dive by yourself," she said. "That's one of the most important rules there is. If you have somebody with you, they will be able to help you if you get into trouble."

One of the other rules was about paying attention to how long you can stay down. "You can get carried away," she warned. "You're enjoying yourself so much that you forget how long you've been underwater and then, all too soon, you discover you've used all your oxygen."

Everybody listened carefully to this briefing. They would never break any of the rules, they thought. Never …

At last it was time to go. They all fitted into one of

the smaller boats that were equipped with outboard engines. Once everybody was on board, Miss Worsfold put the engine into gear and began the crossing to the reef. The water rapidly became shallower, until it was probably not much more than twenty feet deep. It was sandy on the bottom, but now there were coral formations as far as the eye could see, some of them almost reaching up to the surface.

Miss Worsfold stopped the boat. "Time to get your gear ready," she said.

This was quite tricky, but the ten students helped one another to clip their oxygen cylinders onto their backs and to put on their flippers. Then Miss Worsfold inspected everybody to check that no mistakes had been made. "The last thing you want is to discover a problem with your equipment when you're way down below."

Poppy and Amanda Birtwhistle were to be dive partners. Amanda was pleased about this, as Poppy was just the sort of person anybody would like to dive with: she was a good swimmer and, more importantly, she was clear-headed. Poppy never panicked, even in a dangerous situation. There would be no need to be nervous with Poppy at her side.

Yet Amanda was still a bit uneasy as they waited their turn to go into the water. She knew that this was probably not the best time to ask a question about sharks, but she felt that she had to do just that.

"Do you think there are any … any sharks around here?" Amanda tried to make her voice sound normal, but it went high when she got to the word 'sharks'.

"Sharks?" replied Poppy. "Oh, I don't know. Probably not, but there might be."

"Might be?" asked Amanda.

Poppy tried to sound unconcerned. "Well, you can never tell. It's possible, yes …"

Amanda's voice quivered. "Possible that there are sharks?"

Poppy looked at her friend. She did not want to alarm her, but she did not want to lie either. She could say that there were no sharks and that Amanda need not worry, but she knew this would not be the right thing to do. So, as calmly as she could, she said, "There can be sharks *anywhere*, Amanda – anywhere in the sea – and even in some rivers that are close to the sea."

Amanda's voice sounded tiny. "Oh," she said.

"But you have to remember some things about sharks," Poppy went on. "Firstly, sharks are often very shy creatures. Most of the time they don't want to get close to people at all. They keep their distance."

"*Most* of the time?" said Amanda. "That means that *some* of the time they like to get close."

Poppy thought about this. "All right," she said at last. "*Some* sharks are not all that shy."

"Like great whites?" asked Amanda, her lip

trembling at the thought of those large and dangerous creatures.

"Yes," said Poppy. "I wouldn't call them shy. But remember, there are lots of other sharks that are much shyer than great whites. Reef sharks, for instance. They don't attack people – most of the time."

Amanda absorbed this information. "*Most* of the time," she said. "*Most* of the time …"

"And the other thing," Poppy said, "is that sharks usually don't like shallow water, and the water around here is really very shallow, isn't it? Look down there – you can see the sand quite clearly."

Amanda glanced over the side of the boat. She could see the sand at the bottom, but it seemed to her that it was a good way down. There was plenty of swimming room for sharks, she thought.

Ben and Badger were the first to go, rolling backwards into the water the way that divers do. They were followed by Bartholomew Fitzhardy and Thomas Seagrape. Then it was the turn of Poppy and Amanda. Poppy made a thumbs-up sign to Amanda and entered the water with a splash, her friend following a moment later.

The water was wonderfully clear. As Poppy looked around, she was able to see far into the distance, into a vast green world through which light filtered down from the surface. She saw outcrops of coral below her – tiny mountains around which brightly coloured fish swam in lazy shoals, drifting in the flow of water, darting here and there for some tiny scrap of food or to escape from some larger fish. Waving fronds of seaweed made tiny forests in which were hiding cautious, half-hidden sea creatures. She saw a large crab, its pincers held out before it, scuttling sideways across the seafloor. She spotted a fish with a nose like a needle, almost as long as its body, stretching out in front of it.

Amanda stayed close to Poppy, feeling more secure when she had her friend firmly in sight. She was less nervous now and was enjoying the feeling of weightlessness that a diver experiences. At the same time, she was aware that there was a current, and that if she stopped moving her arms and legs she would drift away really rather fast, as if carried in unseen arms.

Poppy pointed to an outcrop of coral that she wanted to examine more closely. Amanda nodded and followed her towards the colourful mound. There were large clumps of seaweed at its base and strange, bulbous formations on its side. A couple of large grey fish, their eyes as big as saucers, watched them from the sides of the coral, their mouths opening and closing as if engaged in conversation.

Both girls were caught up in the fascinating world of the coral reef. Poppy had found a tiny cave – no more than the width of two hands – that some brightly coloured fish were using as a hiding place.

Amanda was watching a school of small striped fish. Neither noticed that slowly but surely the two of them were being separated by the action of the current. Poppy was not moving very much, keeping her position by moving her flippers up and down like paddles. Amanda, however, was drifting along with her school of fish, so absorbed in watching them that she did not notice how far the current was carrying her.

After a few minutes of examining the coral, Poppy turned around to look for Amanda. In a moment of shock, she realised the other girl was not there. Moving away from the coral, she scanned the underwater landscape around her. Not far away she saw two of the boys swimming together towards a coral face. But that was all.

Poppy thought hard. Amanda could not have been gone for more than a few minutes, so she was bound to be somewhere nearby. And then she thought: *If she has drifted away, then she would have gone in the same direction as the current.* Now, by looking at the way in which the fronds of seaweed were floating, Poppy was able to work out where that would be.

But then the thought occurred to her that she should not go off on her own to find Amanda: that would be breaking the rule that you did not dive by yourself. What she should do was to get the two boys she had just seen to join in her search. So, swimming as fast as she could, she made her way over to join them.

The two boys were Thomas and Bartholomew. When they saw her swimming towards them, they waved cheerfully and pointed at the fish they were studying.

It was frustrating for Poppy. One thing you cannot do when you are diving is talk, so Poppy had to communicate by hand signals. Pointing in the direction in which she thought Amanda must have drifted, she made a series of frantic movements with her hands. They had all been taught basic diving signals, but now, in this emergency, Poppy found that she could not remember them. Through their diving masks, Poppy could see at first puzzlement on the faces of Thomas and Bartholomew, but this soon changed to concern. Thomas remembered his signals and made the sign for 'okay' with his fingers and thumb. That prompted Poppy's memory, and she made the action for 'swim in this direction'.

All three were strong swimmers and they were soon shooting through the water, scattering the surprised fish about them. As they went, they scanned the water ahead, hoping to see a line of rising bubbles that would guide them to their missing friend.

It was Thomas who spotted Amanda first. Grabbing hold of Poppy's arm, he made the diving signal for 'look over there' – pointing two fingers, forked into a V. Poppy looked: a short distance away, rising up like a stream of silver, were bubbles of air. And as they got closer, they saw a figure huddled on the sea-bed, in much deeper water. It was Amanda. But what was she doing? From where they were, it seemed that she was struggling with something and was waving her arms frantically.

It took barely a minute for them to reach her, but it was not until they were directly on the scene that they realised that she had been caught by an immense giant clam. This sea creature had closed its wide, serrated shell on a strap of her cylinder harness, and try as she might she was unable to free it.

Thomas was the first to reach Amanda's side. Seeing him, she stopped struggling and pointed to the clam and the strap that was so firmly wedged in its shell. As Poppy and Bartholomew looked on, Thomas pulled as hard as he could on the strap. It would not budge, nor did it make any difference when Bartholomew added his strength and joined the tugging match.

Thomas did some quick thinking. He realised that there would be no way of opening the clam shell – it was far too powerful for its jaws to be prised apart. That meant the strap would have to be cut, and for that he would need a knife. Turning to Poppy, he made a sawing motion with his hands. She understood what he meant and shook her head. Bartholomew did the same. None of them had a knife of any sort, let alone the sort of strong diving knife that would be needed for a task like that.

Thomas thought again. If the strap could not be cut, the only thing Amanda could do would be to abandon her oxygen cylinder altogether. The difficulty with that, of course, is that when you have been deep underwater, you have to swim to the surface slowly and let the body gradually adjust to the change in pressure. If you do not do this, you can get something called 'the bends' – a very dangerous condition that comes about when bubbles form in the blood or muscles. The only way to avoid the bends is to take the journey to the surface very slowly, and that would be Amanda's problem: how could she go up slowly when she had no air to breathe?

These were the thoughts that were going through both Thomas's and Poppy's minds. Poppy wondered how they were going to get around it. And then an answer came to her. It was a simple answer, and she was sure that it would work. Gripping Thomas's arm, she pointed to the strap and then to Amanda's oxygen tank. After that she gestured away from Amanda, hoping to send the message that she should abandon the cylinder. Thomas watched her closely but it was clear he had not yet understood what she meant. So Poppy continued, pointing to her regulator – the mouthpiece through which divers breathe – taking it momentarily out of her mouth and passing it to Amanda before putting it back in her own mouth.

Suddenly, Thomas and Amanda understood. Now all that Thomas had to do was to detach Amanda's air cylinder and then accompany her on a slow ascent to the surface. The first part of that was easier said than done, as complicated fasteners had to be unbuckled, but eventually the oxygen tank fell loose. Amanda was clearly nervous, but Thomas immediately took his regulator from his mouth and offered it to her. Reassured that she would not be left airless, Amanda took a deep breath and began to swim gradually upwards, supported by Thomas on one side and Poppy on the other, with Bartholomew following after. After a few strokes they stopped and Thomas passed his regulator back to Amanda to allow her to take another breath. And so they made their way slowly, but safely, to the surface.

Once they had broken the surface, Amanda gasped in a lungful of fresh air and immediately expelled half of it in a shout of joy.

"Thanks!" she shouted. "You saved my life."

Bartholomew and Poppy laughed. Thomas, who was always modest, shook his head. "No, I didn't. You would have been fine."

Amanda knew this was not true. "No, I wouldn't. I was beginning to panic. I wasn't thinking straight."

Poppy noticed the boat now heading over towards

Ben and Badger were the first to go, rolling backwards into the water the way that divers do.

Amanda took a deep breath and began to swim gradually upwards, supported by Thomas on one side and Poppy on the other . . .

The sea creature had closed its shell on a strap from Amanda's cylinder harness.

them. "Miss Worsfold's on her way," she said.

"Good," said Thomas. "I hope she has a diving knife."

When Miss Worsfold arrived, she helped all four of them into the boat and listened as Poppy gave an account of what happened. "Thomas was the hero," she said. "He saved Amanda."

Miss Worsfold looked at Thomas and smiled. "Well done, Thomas," she said. "That was good thinking. If Amanda had come straight up, she could have got the bends." Then she frowned. "Mind you, there's still a valuable piece of equipment down there – we'll have to do something about that."

Thomas lost no time in volunteering. "I'll go straight down again," he said, "as long as you lend me a diving knife."

Miss Worsfold nodded. "I can, but I think I should come with you."

Poppy's face fell at this. "Couldn't I go with him, Miss Worsfold?"

Miss Worsfold hesitated. But then she said, "Why not? You will be careful, won't you?"

Thomas and Poppy reassured her that they would be very careful. There had been enough emergencies for one day and they did not want to cause another one.

After they had each checked their equipment, they rolled over backwards into the water and began to swim down again to the bottom. The jaws of the clam were still tightly shut. Taking Miss Worsfold's diving knife from its sheath, Thomas soon cut through the nylon strap that was caught in the clam's jaws. Making the 'all okay' signal with his left hand, he retrieved the abandoned oxygen cylinder and he and Poppy slowly returned to the surface, pausing halfway to avoid any chance of the bends.

"Well done," said Miss Worsfold with a smile as they dragged Amanda's oxygen cylinder into the boat. Then her expression changed. "You know, though, I'm going to have to report this incident to Captain Macbeth."

Poppy looked anxious. "But everything worked out all right," she said. "Amanda wasn't hurt – nobody was."

Miss Worsfold frowned. "That's not the point. The Captain has to know about every incident involving safety. That's the rule."

Poppy looked away. Amanda *had* broken the rules by going off on her own. But was she herself partly to blame for not keeping a closer eye on Amanda? She did not want to get Amanda into trouble, but neither did she want to take the blame herself.

She made one last plea to Miss Worsfold. "Can't we just forget about it, Miss Worsfold? Just this time? And I promise you, it'll never happen again."

Miss Worsfold shook her head. "No, Poppy, we

can't," she said. "Rules are not there to be broken. I'm sorry, but I'm going to have to ask both of you to come with me to the Captain's cabin once we get back to the *Tobermory*."

CHAPTER 9

A lie

Fee did not see Poppy again until they were well on their way to Cairns, where the Tall Ships race was due to begin. She found her sitting by herself at the foot of one of the masts, shaded from the sun by the shadow cast by the main boom. Fee saw at once that there was something unusual about the other girl's manner. Poppy was usually cheerful and enthusiastic; now, though, she looked downcast and worried.

Fee sat down next to her friend. "Something wrong?" she asked.

Poppy shook her head. "I'm fine," she said. "I'm just fine."

But Fee could tell that she was not. She wondered whether Poppy was upset at having to say goodbye to her parents in Sydney. You can get used to being away from home – almost to the point of not thinking about it all that much – but then something brings it all back to you and you start to feel homesick. "You can tell me, you know," she said. "Are you missing your mum and dad?"

The question seemed to surprise Poppy, who looked up suddenly. "Missing them? Of course I miss them. Everybody misses home, don't they?"

"So, is that what's making you look so miserable?" asked Fee.

Poppy looked down at the deck once more. It seemed as if she were debating with herself whether or not she should take Fee into her confidence. Then she raised her eyes and Fee could see that she was close to tears.

"It's so unfair," said Poppy. "It wasn't my fault, you know. It wasn't my fault at all."

Fee had heard about the diving incident – news spreads like wildfire on a ship – but she did not know the details. Was this what Poppy was talking about? *But surely Poppy had nothing to do with what happened*, thought Fee. Hadn't it all been to do with Amanda getting caught by a giant clam – or something equally odd?

She waited for a moment to see if Poppy was going to say anything more. When she did not, Fee asked her to tell her exactly what had happened. Was it true that Amanda had almost drowned because her leg had been caught in the jaws of a giant clam?

Poppy frowned and shook her head. "It wasn't like that at all," she said. "I've heard those stories of divers being trapped that way – but it's impossible, you know. It would be hard to fit your leg inside. But you could get a belt or a strap caught. That's what happened to Amanda."

Fee shivered. The idea of being caught so far under water and being unable to get up for air was the very worst kind of nightmare.

"Thomas saved her life, you know," Poppy continued. "We both looked for her and then he shared his air with her while she came up. He was a real hero."

Fee agreed. But why would anybody have blamed Poppy for this? What had it got to do with her? If anything, she deserved to be praised for her part in the rescue.

Poppy explained. "Miss Worsfold told us that we had to report to the Captain," she began. "It seems there's a rule that he has to be told about every incident. So we went along – Thomas, Bartholomew, Amanda and I – and told him what had happened."

"And what did he say?" asked Fee.

"He sat and listened," answered Poppy. "Then he shook his head. Like this." Poppy demonstrated.

"Why?" asked Fee. "Was he cross with you? Because I don't think that he —"

Poppy did not let her finish. "You know how he looks when you've done something you shouldn't?"

Fee did. The Captain had a way of looking disappointed – as if you had somehow let him down. He did not look like that very often because he was a kind man and tried to put people at their ease, but sometimes his irritation showed when it had to.

Poppy continued with her story. "He asked why Amanda was by herself when she saw the giant clam."

"And why was she?" asked Fee. She knew enough about diving to know that you never dived by yourself if you could avoid it.

Poppy replied that she thought Amanda had drifted off because she was not paying attention. "Not that I'm blaming her," she added. "It's really easy to do that if you're looking at fish. You don't realise you're drifting with the current, and before you know it, you're far away."

"So it was her fault," said Fee. "In a way, that is. As you say, it happens quite easily – but it was still her responsibility to pay attention."

Poppy nodded. "I didn't move," she said. "Amanda was the one who allowed herself to drift." She paused. "But she lied about it."

Fee drew in her breath. "What? She said she didn't drift?"

With a further nod of her head, Poppy confirmed what Fee had said. "Before I could say anything, she told the Captain she had signalled to me that she was going off after the fish and that I had signalled back to say I would come too."

"And she didn't?"

"No," said Poppy. "She didn't. I'm absolutely positive she didn't."

Fee asked what happened next.

"I couldn't believe my ears," said Poppy. "I looked at her and she just looked back at me as if daring me to deny it."

"And did you?" asked Fee.

"I tried to," said Poppy. "But then the Captain held up a hand and told me to keep quiet. Then he shook his head again and said that it sounded to him as if we had both failed to pay attention and that we were both to blame."

The unfairness of this shocked Fee. From what she had heard, it was clear that it was all Amanda's fault and Poppy had done no wrong. She was astonished that Amanda Birtwhistle should tell a lie to get herself out of trouble. That was the sort of behaviour one might expect from somebody like Hardtack, not from a girl like Amanda.

"The Captain gave us a lecture," Poppy went on, "about safety. Then he said that as punishment we wouldn't be allowed to dive for the rest of the voyage. He said we were lucky not to have had a tragedy on our hands and he hoped we had learned our lesson."

Fee was eager to hear what Poppy had said to Amanda afterwards.

"When we left the Captain's cabin," Poppy said, "I asked Amanda what she had been thinking about. I told her that what she had said was a complete lie and it had got us both into trouble."

"And what did she say to that?" asked Fee.

"She denied it. She said that she hadn't told any lies and that she had signalled to me and I had signalled back. She said that I must have forgotten." Poppy paused. "But you know what? I don't believe her. She wouldn't look at me when she spoke – that's always a sign of being ashamed."

Fee was silent. Being on board a ship with a lot of other people taught you lots of lessons. And one that she was learning now – and learning very quickly – was that although it is a good thing to trust people, there are times when your trust can be misplaced. Poppy had trusted Amanda, only to discover that the other girl was prepared to make up a false story to get herself out of trouble. *How could anybody do such a thing?* she asked herself. The answer, it seemed, was simply that some people can do things like that quite easily. It made Fee sad to think this, because she wanted the world to be a fair place. But sometimes, she realized, it was anything but fair.

They were now not far from Cairns, and by mid-afternoon the *Tobermory* had sailed into the large bay in front of the town and dropped anchor. The rattling of the great anchor chain as it snaked down into the water was normally a welcome sound as it meant that there would be swimming or exploring, or some other exciting activity. Of course, diving lessons were popular, as Matron had been a champion diver and liked nothing more than to demonstrate her skills and help others master the art of entering the water without too much of a splash.

But as they had sailed into the bay there was something else to attract their attention. There, lined up at anchor and bobbing up and down with the gentle swell, was a fleet of large sailing ships – their competition in the great race that was to start in Cairns and finish at Kangaroo Cliff near Darwin, far away on the northern coast of Australia. Distances are huge in Australia and it would be a long voyage between those two places. Just how long it would take depended not only on the wind, which was unpredictable, but also on the skill of the crew. A strong wind in a favourable direction is not much use if the people on board do not know how to take advantage of it, so a race such as this would be a real test of helming, or steering, the boat, of trimming the sails so they would pick up every ounce of push that the wind gave, of using the currents, and of the crew's ability to keep going day and night, without taking their eye off the task in hand.

Once the anchor had dropped and settled into the sand below, Mr Rigger called the whole company to a meeting on deck. Once all had assembled, the Captain came up from his cabin to address them. He congratulated them on a good voyage – nothing was said about the diving incident – and then went on to point out the other sailing ships at anchor around the bay.

"Every one of these ships," he said, "is a training ship – just like the *Tobermory*. And each of them is crewed by people just like you."

They all looked at the ships across the bay, imagining what the other crews would be like. Fee asked herself whether each would have its equivalent of Hardtack and Co. Would they also have a teacher who could dive as well as Matron or an officer with a moustache like Mr Rigger's?

The Captain was now pointing to the largest vessel in this group of ships, which was flying a large black, red and yellow flag.

"Where's that ship from?" asked the Captain. "Anybody know?"

Ben was not sure, but thought he would guess. "Holland?" he called out. "I think that's the Dutch flag."

It was a perfectly reasonable guess, but it brought a hoot of derision from Geoffrey Shark. "Dutch flag?" he shouted. "You need glasses, MacTavish! Can't you tell the German flag when you see it?"

"Maybe he doesn't know the difference between Holland and Germany," called out Maximilian Flubber.

There was some laughter at this, but not much. Ben glowered back at Shark and Flubber, his ears burning with embarrassment.

"None of that, please!" snapped the Captain. Looking directly at Shark, he continued, "MacTavish made a reasonable suggestion, Mr Shark. But perhaps you'd care to tell us what the flag on that other ship is." He pointed at a ship lying beyond the German vessel. "Well, come on, Geoffrey. You tell us."

Shark's eyes narrowed. "France?" he ventured.

This brought a hoot of laughter from a number of people.

"No," said the Captain. "Wrong. That's a Russian ship." He paused. "So don't be too quick to laugh when other people get things wrong."

Ben felt a bit better now that Shark had been embarrassed too, but there was not much time to think about this as the Captain was now describing the strengths and weaknesses of the other entrants in the race. There were sixteen ships in all, although some of them were too small to pose much of a challenge to the *Tobermory*. The German boat, the *Prince of Hamburg*, would be the main competition. The *Tobermory* should be able to hold its own against the Russian boat, the *Black Sea Belle*, which was heavier and therefore slower than the *Tobermory*. Two other strong competitors were the *Melbourne*, from Australia, and the *Spirit of Hokianga*, from New

Zealand. Although they were sleek and fast, they were smaller and might find the going heavy when faced with rough seas.

"If we want to win," Captain Macbeth continued, "we'll have to give it everything we've got." He paused and looked out over the heads of the ship's company standing before him. "Are you prepared to do that, everyone?"

There was only one answer, and they gave it: "Aye aye, sir!" This was the naval way of saying yes – and they meant it.

With the main business of the meeting over, Bartholomew Fitzhardy asked Captain Macbeth whether they could go swimming. The Captain smiled when he heard the question. "Not if you want to stay alive," he said. "Matron knows why," he added.

Badger looked puzzled, but Matron's response soon made it clear.

"I've been here before," she said. "It was for an international diving competition back in my diving days. And I met a diver then who had a very narrow escape."

They all waited for Matron to say more.

"Crocodiles," she said. "This diver I met had been doing a display of cliff-diving and had a bad shock when she opened her eyes underwater and saw a large crocodile coming straight towards her. She said she had never swum so fast in her life and she got out of the water just in time."

The Captain nodded. "Yes, crocodiles," he said. "I believe I warned you about them before. This is crocodile territory, I'm afraid."

"But this is the sea," Bartholomew protested. "And look, there are plenty of boats about."

The Captain shook his head. "Remember, these are saltwater crocodiles," the Captain reminded him. "Out on the reef it's safe enough, but inshore it's a different matter. It may be rare for them to be in the harbour here, but they could be. And I don't think it's worth taking the risk. So, no swimming until we're well away from these waters."

It was disappointing, as it had been a hot day and people would have welcomed the chance to cool down in the water. But they were sensible and realised that the Captain's advice was good. Or most of them did. Hardtack, who earlier had said that he was not scared of what he called "overgrown lizards", smirked at the Captain's warning and gave his friends Flubber and Shark a knowing look. Poppy noticed it, and whispered to Fee, "I bet they're planning something."

"Who?" asked Fee.

Poppy nodded in the direction of Hardtack and his friends. "Those three."

Fee raised an eyebrow. "Do you think they'd be stupid enough to go swimming here?"

"They might be," said Poppy. "Those three have done some pretty stupid things in their time."

"If they do," she whispered to Poppy, "it could be the last mistake they make."

Poppy sighed. "I wouldn't wish a crocodile attack on anybody, even Hardtack. So I just hope they're not going to do anything dangerous."

Fee said nothing but had a bad feeling that that was exactly what they were going to do.

CHAPTER 10

Dangerous swimming

Poppy found it hard to get to sleep that night. She was finding it difficult to forget what had happened in the Captain's cabin when Amanda Birtwhistle had so unfairly landed her in trouble. It is never pleasant to be punished, but if the punishment is for something you have not done, that it is even worse. Poppy was astonished that Amanda should think she could get away with her story. She could fool others, perhaps – because nobody else had been there – but Amanda must have realised Poppy herself knew the truth. How could Amanda look at herself in the mirror and not cringe with embarrassment at the thought that the face looking back at her was a dishonest one?

Poppy had found herself standing close to Amanda when they were both lining up for dinner in the mess hall. Amanda had avoided her. In fact, she had pretended not to see Poppy at all – and that simply confirmed what Poppy already thought: Amanda was ashamed. And well she might be.

Fee had spotted what was going on. "Amanda's

trying not to look at you," she whispered to Poppy over the dinner table.

Poppy nodded. "I know," she said.

"I wonder if she's going ignore you for the rest of the trip," Fee speculated. "What if you're both on helming duty at the same time? What if you're both turning the wheel together?"

Poppy had to smile. "That could be hard. She would have to pretend she was steering with a ghost."

"Or if you bumped into one another in a passageway," Fee went on, "she'd have to pretend that there was nobody there. Or if you spoke to her …"

"She'd have to act as if she were deaf," interrupted Poppy. "She'd have to ask, 'Did somebody say something?'"

It was all very well, of course, for the two girls to joke about this, but Poppy felt really hurt by what had happened. She toyed with the idea of going back to see the Captain and telling him that what Amanda had said was untrue, but thought this would not make any difference. Captain Macbeth was always prepared to listen, and everybody knew that he was a fair man, but what could he do in these circumstances? He was being given two completely different versions of events and had no way of telling which one was true. No, there was no point in speaking to him.

By lights out, Poppy felt no better. Lying in the dark, she stared up at the cabin ceiling and went over everything in her mind, getting angrier and angrier by the moment. Then she tried not to think about it, but this did not work very well. She thought of where they were – of the other ships in the harbour and the Tall Ships race – but whenever she did Amanda somehow came into the picture. She saw Amanda at the wheel of one of the small boats, looking up at the *Tobermory* and pretending not to see her. She saw Amanda climbing up the rigging of the German training ship, then looking back towards the *Tobermory*, but very deliberately not catching Poppy's eye.

She would have liked to switch on the light and read. That is always a good way of stopping yourself from thinking thoughts you do not want to think, but if she did that she could wake Fee up, and she wanted to avoid that. So Poppy closed her eyes once more and this time tried to think about things that had nothing at all to do with life on the *Tobermory*. She thought of home, of the farm near Alice Springs and of the sheep they gathered for shearing – but then one of the sheep seemed to be avoiding her, and when she looked more closely she saw that its face was remarkably like that of Amanda Birtwhistle …

And it was then that she heard the noise.

At first she thought it was the sound of small waves lapping at the side of the boat. This sound is always present at sea, but at times it becomes louder if the waves grow bigger for some reason. This can be caused by the wake of a passing boat or a sudden gust of wind, but will soon pass. But this time it was different. Somewhere down at the side of the boat, more or less immediately below the porthole of Poppy and Fee's cabin, somebody – or something – was splashing around in the water.

Slipping out of her hammock, Poppy crossed the cabin to investigate. In the darkness, the porthole was a faintly glowing circle. There was a full moon that night, and outside the silver moonlight was dancing on the surface of the water. Poppy strained her eyes, but was unable to see very much other than the sea and, in the distance, the twinkling lights of the sleeping town. Suddenly, she became aware of a figure beside her. Fee had woken up and was now also out of her hammock.

"I heard a noise," said Poppy. And then, apologetically, "I'm sorry if I woke you up, Fee. I didn't mean to."

"I was awake anyway," said Fee. "I heard something too."

Just at that moment they heard the noise again. "There," said Poppy. "Did you hear that?"

Fee nodded. "Yes, it was a sort of splashing sound," she said.

Poppy hesitated. It was strictly against the rules to go up on deck at night without permission. There was a good reason for this: if you went up there in the darkness and fell overboard, nobody would know what had happened. That was a rule that everybody understood and obeyed. Yet what if the splashing sound was being made by somebody who needed help? Surely that would be a good enough reason to break the rules?

Fee must have been asking herself much the same question because when Poppy turned to her she simply nodded her head. "I think we should go on deck and look," Fee whispered.

Together they made their way out of their cabin, taking great care to close the door behind them as quietly as possible. Then they crept along the corridor and up the companionway that would take them out onto the main deck. Nobody saw them and nobody heard them.

The day had been hot, but the air was now a bit cooler. Above their heads, competing with the moonlight, were thousands of tiny stars, and for a moment both girls simply gazed in wonder at the night scene. On the other side of the bay they saw the mast lights of the other ships move gently with the rocking motion of the sea.

Poppy pointed to the side of the ship from which the noise had come. Then, creeping towards the edge of the deck, they peered over the railings. At first they saw nothing, but then, as their eyes became accustomed to the darkness, they made out three shapes in the water.

Poppy gave Fee a nudge. "Somebody's swimming," she whispered.

And then they heard a voice. It was not a loud voice, but it was loud enough for them to make out exactly what was being said.

"Come on, Geoffrey," it said. "Let's swim all the way round the ship."

"All right," came the reply.

And then, "Wait for me," said a third voice.

Poppy and Fee looked at one another in astonishment. There was no mistaking who it was down there in the water: William Edward Hardtack, Geoffrey Shark and Maximilian Flubber.

As Hardtack and his friends began to swim towards the bow of the ship, Poppy touched Fee's elbow and pointed back towards the companionway. Without saying anything, the two girls moved away from the railings.

"What are we going to do?" asked Fee, dropping her voice to a whisper.

Poppy thought for a moment. "They're being really, really stupid," she replied. "Everybody knows that you should never swim in the sea at night. It's the most dangerous time there is. That's when sharks – and saltwater crocs, too – are much more likely to attack."

Fee drew in her breath. "Should we warn them?" she asked.

Poppy thought it unlikely that the boys would listen to them. "I think we should go and wake Mr Rigger," she said. "It's for their own good. They're in real danger."

Fee knew Poppy was right. The girls lost no time in making their way back down the companionway and then along the corridor towards the section of the boat where the staff cabins were. Poppy had brought her small flashlight with her, and now she switched it on to guide them to the door bearing the notice MR RIGGER, FIRST OFFICER. Not caring now how much noise she made, she knocked loudly.

It took another couple of knocks before Mr Rigger appeared at the door, wearing a dark dressing gown with small anchors all over it.

He looked half asleep. "What is it?" he asked drowsily. "What's wrong?"

Poppy did the talking. "Three of the boys are swimming, Mr Rigger. They can't realise how dangerous it is. We thought we should tell you."

Mr Rigger was now fully awake. "Oh no!" he said. "That's extremely dangerous. Where are they?"

Fee explained that they were about to swim right round the ship. This brought another exclamation of alarm from Mr Rigger, who had now retrieved a large and powerful flashlight from a shelf near his door. Then he strode out along the corridor, followed by the two girls.

"You did the right thing to tell me," he said. "Well done, girls."

Once out on the deck, Mr Rigger made his way towards the bow of the boat. Then, leaning over the railings, he shone his flashlight down towards the sea. The beam soon picked up a shape in the water. Then another, and another after that.

"Hardtack!" shouted Mr Rigger. "Shark! Flubber! Get out of the water this instant!"

Caught in the beam of light, Hardtack looked up at the figures on the deck. "But we were only going for a swim, sir," he shouted back. "It was really hot. We needed to cool down."

This only served to make Mr Rigger even angrier. "I said this instant," he called out. "You're in extreme danger."

The mention of danger seemed to have some effect, and the boys started to swim back towards the rope ladder they had slung over the side as fast as they could. Soon they were all clambering up onto the deck, their hair dishevelled, water dripping from their swimming trunks.

"We weren't doing any harm," muttered Hardtack, scowling at the two girls as he spoke.

Mr Rigger lined the three boys up. "I don't think you realise the risk you were taking," he said severely. "Swimming in these waters is forbidden for a reason. And swimming at night even more so."

"There wasn't anything in the water, sir," offered Flubber in an attempt at an excuse. "We didn't see anything."

"Didn't see anything?" exploded Mr Rigger. "That's exactly the point, Flubber. You don't see what's below you in the water. But it sees you, all right! Oh yes, it sees you."

Hardtack said nothing, and neither did Shark and Flubber. But they all shot hostile glances towards Poppy and Fee. Mr Rigger noticed this. "These girls probably saved your lives, you know," Mr Rigger continued. "I think you should thank them. If they hadn't come to get me, you could be inside the stomach of a great white shark by now. Or inside a large saltwater crocodile, for that matter."

Hardtack smirked. "Oh, surely not, sir …"

Mr Rigger did not let him continue. "So, I suggest you thank them," he said.

The boys said nothing.

"Go on," said Mr Rigger, sounding even firmer now. "Thank them," before adding, "and that's an order."

Reluctantly, the boys mumbled their thanks, though neither Poppy nor Fee felt they meant a word of it. Then, having been ordered below, they made their bedraggled way back to their cabins.

Mr Rigger turned to Poppy and Fee. "You two should go back to bed," he said. "And if those boys cause you any trouble, come straight to me."

Poppy and Fee returned to their cabin and climbed into their hammocks. Poppy was tired now and had no difficulty dropping off to sleep. Fee lay awake for a bit longer and then she too dozed off, lulled by the gentle rocking of the ship.

At breakfast the next day Shark scowled at Poppy, but she stared right back at him and he immediately looked away. He was clearly furious at having been caught red-handed during his night-time swim. Afterwards, though, when they were filing up onto the deck for the pre-race briefing, Flubber sidled up to Fee.

"About last night," he muttered. "We were hauled up before the Captain first thing this morning, you know. We had a real telling-off."

Fee braced herself for a threat.

"I want you to know," Flubber went on, "that I'm glad you called Mr Rigger."

Fee could not contain her surprise. She stared at Flubber in astonishment as he explained. "It wasn't my idea," Flubber continued, glancing around him as he spoke. "Bill suggested it."

Bill? It took Fee a moment or two before she realised that Flubber was talking about Hardtack. Somehow, the shortening of his name made him seem much less threatening. But then she thought: *No, names tell you nothing about what a person is really like.*

"Hardtack?" Fee asked. "Are you talking about him?"

Flubber nodded. "Yes. He said he was feeling hot and wanted to cool down. I reminded him that we'd been told not to swim, but he said that was all nonsense. He said that he'd seen people swimming off the beach earlier on, and if they could do it, then why couldn't we?"

"Maybe it's safer close to the shore," said Fee. "If the water's shallow, you can see the crocodiles."

"Maybe," said Flubber. "Anyway, Geoff wanted to go too, so I felt I couldn't say anything. They'd think I was a coward if I refused to go."

He looked at her pleadingly, as if he wanted her support, and for a few moments Fee thought of what it must be like to be Flubber and to worry about what Hardtack and Shark thought of you. She looked at him and realised she actually felt sorry for him. *Nobody is completely bad. Even William Edward Hardtack*, she told herself, *must have some good points.* Flubber, certainly, seemed nowhere near as unpleasant as he was.

"You must have felt scared down there in the water," she said.

Flubber looked at her with gratitude. He seemed relieved that here was somebody who understood.

"I was petrified," he confided. "All the time while Bill and Sharky were splashing around, I was thinking

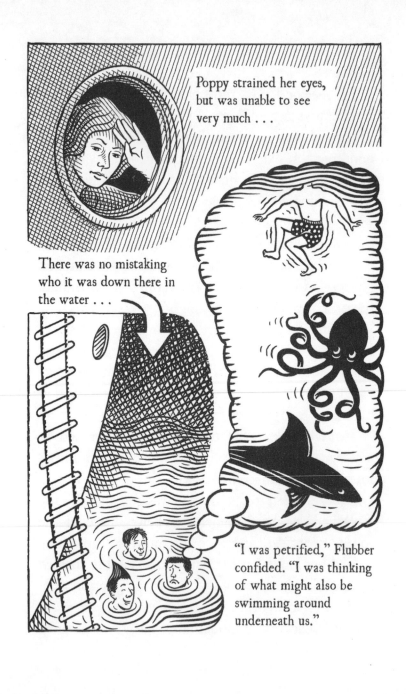

Poppy strained her eyes, but was unable to see very much . . .

There was no mistaking who it was down there in the water . . .

"I was petrified," Flubber confided. "I was thinking of what might also be swimming around underneath us."

of what might also be swimming around underneath us. I tried to keep my legs up as much as possible so that if there was something there it would get to their legs before mine." He paused before he continued, "I know that makes me sound bad, but that's the way it was."

"Don't feel bad," Fee said. "They were the ones who wanted to go. You were ... you were ..." She searched for the right words. She wanted to say, *You were the one who was easily led*, but she realised that this would make him sound weak. Poor Flubber! Why could he just not get away from the influence of the other two? Why couldn't he simply have nothing to do with them?

Flubber found the words for her. "I was the weak one," he said miserably. "I know I shouldn't do everything they tell me to, but it's hard, you know."

Fee felt even sorrier for him now.

"And what I wanted to say," Flubber continued, "is that I'm very grateful for what you did. I think we really were in danger."

Fee was about to tell him she was glad that she and Poppy had been able to help, but before she could do so Geoffrey Shark appeared and muttered something to Flubber. Fee did not catch what it was, but she saw its effect: Flubber immediately turned away and went off with the other boy.

Poppy had seen Flubber talking to Fee and came

over to ask her what it had all been about.

"So what did Flubber have to say?" she enquired.

"He wanted to thank us," Fee answered. "He was really scared in the water."

Poppy thought about this. Of the three boys, Flubber was definitely the least obnoxious. He had a reputation for lying, but for all anybody knew he might be capable of changing. She had known people who had taken a good hard look at their faults and had done something about them. Perhaps Flubber was beginning to do just that.

"Perhaps we should try to be more friendly to Flubber," Poppy said.

Fee made a face.

"Yes, I know," said Poppy. "But maybe we should give him a chance."

Fee realised that Poppy was right. Friendship with somebody you don't like can be hard, but she knew it was sometimes what you have to do. "We could try," she said.

"Let's do that," said Poppy. "And then we could see if Shark too could be persuaded to show his good side."

Fee raised her eyebrows. "Some things are very, very unlikely," she said.

"It might be worth a go," Poppy mused. "And if you don't try something, how will you ever know if it's possible?"

Fee had to agree on that, but she wondered if Ben and Badger would think so too.

"Well," said Poppy, "it's exactly the same thing: if you don't ask them, you won't find out."

Their conversation ended on that note. The Captain had now arrived and they needed to pay attention to what he had to say.

"In half an hour," the Captain announced, "the Tall Ships race will begin. I've looked at the weather forecast for the next week or so, and I'm happy to say the wind is in a favourable direction and will be fairly strong. That means we have some very exciting sailing ahead of us, everyone."

Now he unrolled a large chart on which he pointed out the route from the starting point of the race to the final destination. The voyage would take them up to the easterly tip of Australia, the Cape York Peninsula, and then across the wide Gulf of Carpentaria to a bay at the foot of Kangaroo Cliff.

"The first ship to reach Kangaroo Cliff," he said, "wins the race."

Poppy and Fee exchanged excited glances. Ben, who was standing nearby, smiled at them and asked them whether they thought the *Tobermory* might win. Poppy laughed. "Of course," she said.

Fee was more cautious. "I hope so," she said.

The Captain now gave detailed instructions. Ben and Badger were on helming duty for the first two hours, while Poppy and Fee were charged with handling some of the sheets – the ropes that controlled the sails. Thomas was to help with navigation, as were Tanya and Angela. Others were detailed to raise the anchor, keep the mainsail in trim and climb up the mast to keep a look-out. Everybody had their duties and was determined to do them to the best of his or her ability, even if it was something as simple as helping Cook to peel potatoes for lunch.

Lunch, though, was a long time away and nobody was thinking of that just yet. They had a race to begin. That was quite enough for the time being.

CHAPTER
11
Boy on the island

The start of the race was marked by the firing of a small cannon from the deck of an Australian naval ship. As soon as they heard the cannon and saw the small puff of smoke that accompanied its firing, all hands on the *Tobermory* gave a loud cheer. There was cheering too from the crews of the other ships, and commands were shouted in many different languages as sails were tightened and the sleek hulls of the ships surged forwards, cutting their way through the waves, throwing up clouds of foam and spray.

The *Melbourne* led the way. The Australian boat seemed to pick up a favourable wind within a minute or two of the starting cannon, shooting ahead of its nearest rival, the *Prince of Hamburg*. After that came the *Spirit of Hokianga* and one of the smaller ships, an Italian boat called the *Napoli*. It was disappointing for the students on the *Tobermory* to find themselves lagging behind, but as Mr Rigger pointed out as he went round the deck checking up on everybody, "A race isn't over until it's finished, and that's many, many days away."

The next few days were something of a blur in the memory of most members of the *Tobermory* crew. A fully rigged sailing ship, moving at top speed in a strong wind, can be like a galloping horse. It must be carefully controlled all the time – held in check one moment, while being allowed to shoot ahead the next. Not only must the sails be coaxed into just the right shape, to take advantage of every breath of wind, but a sharp eye must be kept on what the sea itself is doing. Where are the waves coming from? How big are they? Will they help the ship along or will they hinder her by making her wallow in the troughs between their crests?

It was demanding work, and while they were racing along there was no time for lessons. This meant that the normal routine of a school ship was suspended, just as it was during the official school holidays. But this was no holiday for the students of the *Tobermory*. The day was divided into watches, and every minute of every watch involved hard work – tugging at ropes, keeping the deck clear, struggling with the helm as the ship fought with the action of wind and wave. At the end of their watches, most people were utterly exhausted and would collapse into their hammocks for some much needed rest.

At night the pace continued, as they were in the open sea and there was no place to drop anchor and spend the hours of darkness getting their breath back.

The night hours, too, were divided into watches. Those whose watches fell during the small hours of the morning had to be woken, get dressed and report on deck, no matter how tired they felt.

When Ben and Badger were on night watch, Ben would set his alarm for ten minutes before they were due to start their duties. Then, when the buzzer sounded and he had rolled himself out of his hammock, he would cross to Badger's side of the cabin to wake his sleeping friend.

Badger was a sound sleeper and was sometimes difficult to rouse. You cannot actually turn over in a hammock – or not very easily – but he would try to do that, just as you might turn over in a bed and bury your head under a pillow when somebody comes to wake you up.

"Come on, Badge," Ben would say. "Time to go on watch."

From within the twisted hammock there would come an indistinct murmur: "Still sleeping," or "Not morning yet," or something of that sort.

To which Ben would reply, "Ten minutes to watch. Come on!"

Reluctantly, Badger would open his eyes and unwind himself from the comfortable embrace of his hammock. And so the watch would begin, with a number of still half-asleep people silently going about their duties under a wide and empty sky. But as they woke up fully, they would all be caught up in the sheer wonder of what they were doing. There they were, sailing across a wide expanse of sea with only the wind and the waves to accompany them. There they were in the darkness, under the great velvet canopy of the night sky, with the stars glittering high above them, tiny specks of light that went on and on and on in uncountable numbers.

Even during the day, when the sky was filled with light and the sun played on the waves, the sea was still a lonely place. Now and then they saw a ship in the distance, making its way to one of the ports further south. Occasionally they saw a lone yacht on the horizon, but for most of the time there was nothing but ocean in every direction. Of the other Tall Ships – their competitors in the race – there was no sign, although every so often somebody would imagine they could make out masts and sails in the far distance.

"How do you think we're doing?" Ben asked Mr Rigger a few days after the race had started. "Do you think we're in the lead?"

Mr Rigger smiled and shrugged his shoulders. "I have no idea, Ben," he replied. "All I know is that we could be first, second, third, or fourth. Or sixteenth. Does that answer your question?"

Ben laughed. "I suppose it does, sir," he replied.

The Captain spoke to the whole school each

morning and showed the crew where they were on the chart. He could be quite sure of this from his instruments. GPS will show you exactly where you are anywhere on the surface of the Earth, but Captain Macbeth still liked to use the old methods of finding their position. By plotting how long they had been sailing and at what speed, he was able to estimate how many nautical miles the *Tobermory* had covered, and from that he could work out exactly where they were.

Looked at on the chart, their progress seemed painfully slow. But that was because Australia is so big and their route so long. Gradually, though, they inched their way closer to the tip of the continent.

Their route had taken them far out to sea, but now that they were nearing Cape York they were much closer to land off their port side. It is a remote and lonely part of the country. There are a few towns and harbours, but these are separated from one another by long distances and the land is rough and impenetrable. In these parts, you can drive for hours along one of the rough tracks and not see a single other person. And you have to be careful: if you stray off the track into the bush, you can very quickly lose your way and never be seen again. It is not the sort of place for people who do not know what they are doing.

The coast is just as deserted, with long miles of empty beaches backed by dense forest. There are cliffs and outcrops of jagged rocks that jut out into the sea;

there are river mouths that give a glimpse of thick vegetation along the banks beyond. There are distant, mysterious hills, shimmering in the heat. If you ever wanted to imagine the very edge of the world, this is what you might see in your mind's eye.

On the morning of the day they got closer to land, Ben and Badger were on look-out duty. This involved climbing up the main mast to the small platform known as the crow's nest. Not everybody liked going up there – and those who had no head for heights would be excused by Mr Rigger and given some other duty. But Ben and Badger both liked being high up and enjoyed the view that the crow's nest afforded.

Their job as look-outs was to see if there were any hidden reefs. The water here is shallow, and although the charts mark the main rocks, there are always obstacles that the chart-makers might have missed. It is possible, too, that there could be small boats that those manning the helm might miss but which would be visible from up high. These boats belonged to local fishermen from the small communities who live in this lonely place. They are not many in number, but they have lived there for thousands of years and they know every inch of this vast territory.

It was Ben who saw something first, as they were sailing past the mouth of a wide bay. In the middle of the bay he noticed there was a small island, and that there was something on it. At first he thought that it might be an animal, but then, as he squinted against the glare, he saw that it was a person, who seemed to be waving their arms to attract attention.

"Look over there," said Ben. "There's somebody on that little island, Badger."

Badger had a pair of binoculars slung around his neck and he now raised these to get a better view. "Yes, you're right," he said.

"What's he doing there?" asked Ben.

Badger looked again. With the motion of the ship, it was difficult to see clearly, but after a moment he slipped the strap over his head and handed the binoculars to Ben. "See what you think, Ben," he said. "I'd say he's waving for help."

Ben looked at the island and the small figure on the sand at its edge. "Yes," he said. "I think you're right, Badge. We should tell Mr Rigger."

Badger cupped his hands and shouted as loudly as he could: "Mr Rigger! Mr Rigger!"

Down on the deck below, Mr Rigger looked up to the crow's nest. He had been teaching a small group of students how to take compass bearings, but a warning from the look-outs took priority over everything else.

Mr Rigger cupped his hands around his mouth and shouted back, "What is it?"

"Somebody on that island," replied Badger at the top of his voice. "He's signalling to us."

Mr Rigger went to the side of the deck and looked over. He could see the island in the distance, but from where he was standing he could not see anybody on it.

"Are you sure?" he shouted up to Badger.

"Yes," yelled Badger. "We're sure."

Now Mr Rigger did not hesitate. "Alter course twenty degrees to port," he called to Angela Singh and Thomas Seagrape, who were on helm duty.

"Altering course," they responded in unison. "Twenty degrees to port."

The great ship's bow swung round obediently and soon the *Tobermory* was heading directly for the island, cutting through the shallow green water at a speed that would bring them to their destination within fifteen minutes or so. Aware that something was happening, those who were not on duty massed up at the bow of the boat, interested in seeing what it was that had caused them to change course.

Mr Rigger called Captain Macbeth from his cabin. The Captain now went to the helm and stood beside Angela and Thomas, ready to take over should he have to. As he stood there, he gave orders for some of the sails to be rolled up so that the *Tobermory* would be slowed down by the time they neared the island. He also ordered the engine to be started so that the ship could be more easily manoeuvred.

"Look-outs down from the crow's nest," he

shouted to Ben and Badger. "And well done for spotting this."

Ben and Badger both felt proud, as a compliment from the Captain was much sought after.

"I hope that person on the island wasn't just waving to say hello after all," muttered Badger. "We'll look a bit silly if he was."

Ben shook his head. "No, I think he really does need help," he said.

As the *Tobermory* drew closer to the island, Ben and Badger were able to see that they were right. It was now clear that the figure on the island was a boy, and that he was very pleased that they were coming to the rescue. Although he had stopped waving his arms, he was pacing up and down anxiously. When they lowered one of the liberty boats, he immediately pointed out a safe place for the boat to land.

As they were the ones who had spotted the boy, Ben and Badger had been chosen to row the boat that would take Mr Rigger and Matron ashore. Matron brought her first aid case, just in case the boy needed medical treatment, and Mr Rigger took a large bottle of water in case the castaway was thirsty.

As they approached the beach, the boy waded into the surf to help guide the boat ashore. They saw that he was a local boy, probably a member of one of the groups whose land this is. These are Aboriginal

The coast is deserted, with long miles of empty beaches backed by dense forest . . .

"Look over there," said Ben. "There's somebody on that little island."

The boy waded into the surf to help guide their boat ashore.

people, who have lived in Australia for many thousands of years and who still speak the first languages ever to have been used on this great continent. They are hardy people, with the skills and knowledge to survive in conditions that would have defeated many others.

The boy greeted them in English.

"Thank you for coming," he said, as he helped to haul the boat onto the sand.

Mr Rigger introduced them. "My name is Rigger," he said. "This is Matron, and these two here are Ben and Badger. They're the ones who saw you waving."

The boy looked at Ben and Badger and grinned. "I'm glad you did," he said. "And my name is … well, I won't give you my full name because you won't be able to say it easily. A lot of people call me Will, and you can do that, if you like."

Ben looked at Will. He was about the same age as Badger and him, he thought.

"So what's the trouble?" asked Mr Rigger. "How did you get stranded out here?"

Will pointed out to sea. "I tied my boat to a rock at the edge of the beach and when the tide came in, it drifted off. I didn't notice it until it was too late, and now it must be miles away."

Mr Rigger nodded. He had seen this happen before, though not in such an isolated place. "I imagine it's gone for good," he said.

Will nodded. He had been smiling, but now his face fell. "It's my own fault," he said.

Mr Rigger tried to make him feel better. "Every one of us has made a mistake," he said. "There won't be a single person at sea who hasn't done something stupid at some point."

Will cheered up when he heard this. "It was an old boat," he said. "It used to belong to my grandfather, but he doesn't need it any more. It's not the end of the world."

Mr Rigger now asked Will why he had come out to the island.

"To meet the plane," Will replied.

Mr Rigger looked confused. "The plane?"

"Yes," said Will. "There's a seaplane that comes here every other month. It brings medical supplies for our people."

They waited for him to continue.

"You see," Will went on, "our people live over there." He pointed to some hills in the distance beyond the shore. "It's very remote, and there are no roads. There's a landing strip, but in the wet it's just a field of mud and nothing can land there."

Matron looked puzzled. "In the wet?" she asked.

Will smiled. "The rainy season," he said. "We call it the wet. Most of the roads and tracks are blocked by mud."

Badger remembered that Poppy had said something about this. She had told him how heavy rains could turn a dry plain into a lake in a matter of minutes.

Will continued his story. "I usually come out to the island to pick up supplies," he explained. "But a couple of days ago, when I came out here, I was late. I got the times mixed up, so when I arrived I saw the plane flying off into the distance. They must have thought I'd forgotten to come."

"Will it come back?" asked Ben.

Will shook his head. "Not until next time," he said. "And that will be two months from now." He paused. "Unless we can get in touch with them."

Will looked expectantly at Mr Rigger, who immediately understood what Will meant.

"We have a radio," said Mr Rigger. "Would you like—"

Will did not let him finish. "Oh, yes please!" he interrupted. "That's just what we need. If I could get in touch with the Flying Doctors, maybe they can send the plane. It could be here by tomorrow."

Matron smiled. She knew all about the Flying Doctor service – the organisation that sends doctors by plane to the remotest parts of Australia where there are no hospitals or surgeries. "I'm sure we'll be able to do that," she said. "Won't we, Mr Rigger?"

Mr Rigger nodded. "No problem," he said. "Let's get back to the *Tobermory* straight away." He turned to Will. "Come with us, Will, so you can speak to them. Then you can stay with us on board overnight."

At these words Ben started to think. They were meant to be in a race, and yet here was Mr Rigger saying that they would spend the night here. How could they possibly do that if they were to have any chance of winning? He wondered whether he should ask Mr Rigger about this, but something held him back. Will needed help, and it was one of the first rules of the sea that you never refuse help to somebody in need. Somebody like Mr Rigger, who had been brought up on the rules of the sea, would know that as well as he knew the alphabet.

When they arrived back aboard the *Tobermory*, there was a large crowd on deck to welcome them. Badger thought that Will might have been nervous about meeting so many new people, but he did not seem in the least bit concerned. With a broad smile on his face, he climbed up the rope ladder onto the deck and shook hands with the Captain, who was waiting to greet him.

Henry seemed particularly pleased to have Will on board. Barking with excitement, he leapt up to lick Will's face, much to the amusement of all those watching.

Poppy was keen to find out what had happened. "Was he shipwrecked?" she asked Badger.

Badger told her about Will's boat drifting away.

Then he went on to explain that Will was hoping to get the seaplane to come the next day and that they would be staying where they were until then.

"But what about the race?" asked Thomas Seagrape, who had been listening to their conversation.

Badger shrugged. "We'll just have to try to catch up later on," he said.

Thomas looked astonished. "But we can't do that," he said. "We've come all this way …"

He did not finish. Captain Macbeth was clapping his hands together, a sign for everybody to gather round him.

"As you will have noticed," he announced, "we have carried out a rescue. According to the law of the sea, it is your duty – as I hope you all know – to help anybody in peril at sea." He paused, looking out over the expectant faces of the crew. "Not only that," Captain Macbeth continued, "but in this case we are offering some additional assistance. We shall be staying here to wait for some urgent medical supplies."

This brought a chorus of surprised – and disappointed – murmuring, but the Captain simply raised a finger and continued. "I know many of you will be upset that we'll be losing valuable time, but we are doing this because it is the right thing to do. I hope everybody agrees."

There was complete silence, though William

Edward Hardtack looked angry and Geoffrey Shark went so far as to sneer – but only behind a raised hand. Then Poppy spoke. "I think it's exactly the right thing to do," she said. "We understand, Captain."

Captain Macbeth smiled at her. "I'm glad you said that, Poppy. You're an Australian and I think you understand how important it is to help people when you're in a remote spot."

Geoffrey Shark looked at Poppy and gave a snigger. "Is he your boyfriend?" he asked under his breath, but just loud enough for Poppy to hear. "This guy we picked up – is he your boyfriend."

Poppy pretended not to hear. She had decided that this was the best tactic with somebody like Shark. If she pretended not to hear, he would be denied the pleasure of learning she was upset by what he had said.

After the Captain's announcement, Mr Rigger took Will down to the radio room, where a call was put through to the Flying Doctor service. After they had been told what had happened, they agreed that the seaplane would return the next morning with the medical supplies.

Will was overjoyed at the news, and even more so when Mr Rigger assured him that they would make a boat available to take him ashore with the supplies as well as food and water for the journey back to his people.

"And now," said Mr Rigger, "you have a bit of time to look around our ship. You'll join us for dinner and we'll find a hammock for you to sleep in tonight."

Will enjoyed his dinner – he sat between Poppy and Badger – and afterwards they all played a game of cards. Then, when the time came to go to bed, a spare hammock was found and hung up in Ben and Badger's cabin. Lights out seemed to come far too soon, and the three boys continued to talk well into the night, telling one another about their different lives. Will was interested to hear what Badger said about his home in New York. It was about as different as could be from the remote spot where his own people lived. As Badger listened to Will tell them about his hunting dogs and his canoe, he found himself thinking how he would happily exchange everything he had for the sort of life that Will led. You could not keep hunting dogs in New York, nor could you throw a boomerang, or fish from the beach, or ride on the back of a turtle. And Ben, listening with equal fascination to Will, found himself in complete agreement as he drifted off to sleep.

CHAPTER 12

Where's Henry?

The seaplane arrived shortly after breakfast the next morning. At first it was no more than a distant drone and a speck in the sky to the south, but a few minutes later everybody had a good view of it as it dropped down onto the bay, bounced about a bit as its floats engaged with the surface of the water and then taxied to a halt beside the *Tobermory*.

Mr Rigger supervised the lowering of the liberty boat that would collect the precious cargo of medical supplies. Will was to row this boat, he said, and he could take Ben and Badger to give him a hand. Poppy could go too, if she wished.

Will and his new friends set off. A short row brought them to the side of the plane, where they tied the boat to a ring on one of the plane's floats. The pilot greeted them cheerfully, laughing as Will apologised for having arrived late the day before. "Easily done, Will," he said, before adding, "and sorry to hear about that boat of yours. You would have been in real trouble if these people hadn't been sailing past."

It did not take long to unload the supplies. Once that was done, the pilot helped them untie their boat, and then stood on one of the floats to wave to them as they rowed back to the *Tobermory*. Joining the others on the deck, Ben, Badger, Poppy and Will watched as the plane took off, bumping at speed across the bay before lifting itself off the surface of the water. Once aloft, the plane circled the *Tobermory*, dipping its wings in salute before climbing up into the sky and disappearing out of sight.

Will had brought an empty backpack with him, and it was in this he now carefully packed the boxes of medicine.

"We'll take you ashore now, Will," Mr Rigger said. "Would you like anybody to come with you to say goodbye?"

Will looked around him. "I'd like Ben and Badger to come," he said. "And Poppy too."

Poppy added her voice. "Can Fee come as well?" she asked.

Mr Rigger nodded. "That's fine," he said.

"And one more," Will suddenly added.

Mr Rigger smiled. "No problem with that," he said. "Who's it to be?"

Will pointed to Henry. "The dog," he said simply. "Can the dog come for the ride?"

Henry could tell he was being talked about and began to wag his tail enthusiastically.

Mr Rigger smiled. "I don't see why not," he replied. "Right," he continued in a business-like manner, "let's get going."

All six of them – seven counting Henry – stepped aboard the rowing boat. Ben and Badger took their place at the oars – they were both experienced rowers – while Mr Rigger took the tiller in order to steer the boat. Will, who was familiar with the waters of the bay, made for the bow so that he could guide them through the rocks near the beach. Poppy and Fee sat amidships, with Henry between them. Fee held his collar just in case he got too excited and tried to jump into the water for a swim.

The tide was with them, and it didn't take long to get to the beach. When they arrived, Will jumped out into the surf and pulled the boat ashore. Then the rest of them disembarked. Henry, who was pleased to be back on dry land, dashed around the beach, chasing his tail, barking with delight.

Will pointed to the thick band of trees which backed onto the beach and explained that although it looked like an impossible barrier, there was a path through. If he followed that, he would arrive home by sunset.

"By sunset?!" exclaimed Mr Rigger "That's hours from now. Are you sure you're going to be all right?"

Will nodded. "I've done this trip hundreds of times," he said. "I know this country well."

As he spoke, a flock of large coloured birds rose from the trees with a raucous squawking.

"Galahs," said Poppy, pointing to the birds as they rose up in the sky.

"Noisy fellows," said Will.

Ben had never seen birds like these before, and he watched in fascination. Everything about Australia was so colourful – and so different. And there seemed to be constant birdsong, filling the air and echoing up into the empty sky. *I like this country*, he said to himself. *I like it very much.*

Mr Rigger suggested that they walk with Will as far as the path through the trees. Then they would say goodbye to him and make their way back to the *Tobermory*. Badger felt sad; he liked Will and it seemed a pity to be losing a new friend so soon after meeting him. But that is part and parcel of living on a boat. You meet all sorts of people in the places you stop in, but you always have to say goodbye and move on. It sometimes seemed to Badger that life was one goodbye after another. If only you could stop the world for a little while and be in the same place with the same friends, doing the same thing for just a little bit longer. But that, he knew, is not the way things are.

While Badger was deep in these thoughts, Poppy suddenly noticed that Henry was no longer with them.

The seaplane taxied to a halt beside the *Tobermory*.

As Will spoke, a flock of colourful birds rose from the trees with a raucous squawking.

"I think we should look and see what the sand has to tell us," Will said.

"Anybody seen Henry?" she asked.

Ben looked around. "He was here a moment ago," he said.

"I saw him too," said Badger. "But now ..."

Mr Rigger reached into his pocket and took out his bosun's whistle. Raising it to his lips, he blew three shrill blasts and then looked out across the beach. "Henry always answers to that," he said. "It never fails. He thinks it means biscuits."

But this time it did fail. They waited for several minutes, and when there was still no sign of Henry, Mr Rigger blew the whistle once more. Again, Henry failed to appear.

Will had an idea. "I think we should look and see what the sand has to tell us," he said. "It'll have a clear enough story to tell."

It was the obvious thing to do, and they all walked behind Will as he began to track the dog's paw prints across the beach.

"He headed towards the trees," said Will. "Maybe he saw something – a kangaroo or a wallaby. He might have gone after it."

They reached the point where the sand ended and the trees began. Sure enough, there were Henry's telltale paw-prints following the path through the trees. Will pointed them out to Mr Rigger and then asked him what he thought they should do.

Mr Rigger frowned. "I suppose we could wait and

see if he comes back," he suggested.

"But he might not," said Poppy. "If he's chasing a roo or something, he could easily get lost."

Will agreed that this was a danger. "Even our own dogs sometimes get lost in this heavy bush," he said, pointing to the thick vegetation. "And a dog who doesn't know this place is even more likely to lose his way."

Mr Rigger rubbed his chin thoughtfully. "But we can't all wander off into the forest," he said. "They're expecting us back at the ship. If we don't turn up soon they'll send out a search party and ..."

" ... and the search party itself could get lost," added Poppy. "That happened once at Alice Springs. They had to send out a search party to find the search party."

Ben thought about this for a moment. "And if the second search party got lost too," he said, "then I suppose they'd have to send out a third search party to look for the second search party ..."

Badger had an idea. "Why don't you go back to the *Tobermory*, sir?" he said to Mr Rigger. "You can tell the Captain that we've gone to look for Henry and then come back for us."

Mr Rigger looked doubtful. "But I don't want you getting lost," he said. "You don't know this land."

"But I do," said Will. "I was born here. I know it like the back of my hand."

Poppy was nodding her head in agreement. "And I know a bit about the bush too," she said. "Remember, I come from Alice Springs."

Mr Rigger was reluctantly won over. "All right," he said. He looked at his watch. "How long do you need?"

They all looked at Will, who looked up at the sun and then scratched his head. "It depends on how far he's gone. I'll have to set off for our place soon so that I can get home by dark. So, if you come back in an hour, we should be here with Henry – with any luck."

Mr Rigger agreed to this and they all made their way back to the boat. Once it had been pushed out into the water, he prepared the oars and started to row. "Good luck," he called out as the boat nosed into the surf and began to pull away from the shore.

"Right," said Will, taking command of the situation, "everyone follow me."

They fell into line behind him. Poppy, being the most experienced bush-walker after Will, took her place at the end of the line, where she would be able to keep an eye open for any dangers that might be lurking behind them. This is one of the key rules when you are in the bush. Everything might be all right in front, but it can be a different matter altogether behind. For all you know, something could be stalking you, and unless you turn around from time to time to check, you might never know it was there.

They walked for about twenty minutes before Will suddenly held up a hand and brought them to a halt.

"Hold on, everybody," he called out. "Henry left the track here."

They crowded round as Will pointed to the place where the dog's prints veered off deeper into the bush.

"What happened here?" asked Ben.

Will shrugged his shoulders. "I suppose something distracted him," he suggested. "Or he went off after whatever it was he had been following."

They waited for Will to say more as he shaded his eyes from the sun, scanning the horizon for any sign of Henry.

"What should we do now?" asked Fee.

"We must carry on looking for him," said Poppy. "We can't leave him out here." She glanced around for support and saw that Ben and Badger were both nodding their heads in agreement.

"But if we do that, we'll have to go off the track," Fee pointed out, "and we could easily get lost."

"But Will knows his way round here," argued Badger. He turned to Will. "You know where we are, don't you, Will?"

Will hesitated. "Yes," he said. "And I've never got lost before."

Fee looked anxious. "But there's always a first time."

"I vote we carry on looking," said Ben. "Will's good

at tracking. You'll be able to follow Henry's paw-prints, won't you, Will, just like you've been doing up till now?"

Will said that he should be able to do that, although it depended on the nature of the ground. If it became muddy it would be a different matter. It also depended on whether there had been any other animals around – a troop of kangaroos would quickly make tracking impossible because they would obscure Henry's paw-prints.

Although Fee had her doubts, the others all agreed that they should continue to look for Henry, and that was what they did. With Will at their head, they began to make their way slowly across a wide stretch of grassland that was punctuated here and there by clumps of tall trees. It was difficult going, as the land was rough and there were many potholes and places where the ground fell away into riverbeds that were dry now, but which during the rainy season – 'the wet' as he had explained to them before – would fill with water. Nobody wanted to show fear, though all of them – with the exception of Will – felt anxious about what they were doing. Taking it in turns to call out for Henry, their voices sounded small and insignificant in the middle of this wild and empty place.

"I wish we could go back," muttered Fee under her breath.

"Are you all right?" asked Ben, who was walking beside her.

"Not really," she whispered. "But don't tell the others."

Poppy, though, had overheard, and was worried about Fee. "Listen, Will," she said. "Perhaps we should get back to the beach. Once Mr Rigger returns, we can ask him what to do."

"And Henry might find his way back by himself," said Ben. "Dogs often do that, you know."

Will thought for a moment. "If that's what you want," he said.

"I think it is," said Poppy. "We've been calling and calling, and there's still no sign of him."

Will did not argue. "All right," he said. "Let's turn round."

And it was at that moment that Badger spotted something that made his heart miss a beat.

"What's that?" he said, pointing to a dark shape in the distance.

Will looked where Badger was pointing. "Oh no . . ." he muttered. And then, once again, "Oh no . . ."

It was clear to everybody that Will was worried. Up until then, he had seemed confident, but now they saw his expression change. It showed fear, and it was unmistakeable.

CHAPTER
13
Crocodiles

The thing that Badger had seen was long and dark, and it had now moved slightly.

"What is it?" asked Badger. "It's hard to see from this distance."

"A croc!" said Will. "There's a creek full of them over there."

The others all peered at the distant shape. It might easily be missed, or might be mistaken for a fallen tree trunk, but now that Will had identified it, it was easier to see what it really was. Ben, who had brought a pair of binoculars with him, was able to get a better view. "It's a long way off," he said. "And it doesn't seem to be in a hurry to go anywhere."

Will shook his head. "He'll know we're here," he said. "We're upwind of him and crocs have a very good sense of smell."

"What do we do?" asked Poppy.

"We move away as fast as we can," said Will.

"Should we run?" asked Ben.

"Just follow me," Will said. "We'll have to get back

to the track by a different route – that croc is blocking our way."

They set off with Will in the lead again. The rough ground stopped them from going quickly, but nevertheless they made good progress. When they stopped, though, to see what the crocodile was doing, they saw that the distance between them and the large creature had shrunk considerably.

"It's following us. Those fellows move fast, even on dry land," said Will. "They don't look as if they can run quickly, but you'd be surprised." He paused. "Okay, everybody, let's get going again."

He took a few steps and then stopped, calling out to everybody to stand still.

"What's wrong now?" asked Poppy.

Will lowered his voice. "There's another one," he said. "Just ahead of us. Look."

They all stared at the shape in the grass ahead of them. Will was right: an extremely large crocodile had appeared from a ditch and was staring back at them.

Will looked about him frantically. "All right, everybody. See those two trees over there?" he said, pointing to two large trees that were growing nearby.

"Yes," said Poppy. "Should we climb them?"

"Yes," said Will. "We've got no choice. But don't run. Just walk very quietly and very slowly towards them. We don't want to disturb that big fellow ahead of us. He's watching."

The chilling words struck fear into each and every one of them. Ben thought to himself, *Please don't let me die, please don't let me die.* Fee thought, *We shouldn't have come out here – I should have known better.* And Poppy and Badger, in their terror, thought similar things.

They did as Will ordered, each of them moving as carefully as they could. At one point the large crocodile closer to them slithered forward, sizing up his prey.

When they reached the first of the trees, Will said, "Ben and Badger, you take this tree. Climb up as high as you can. I'll help Fee and Poppy up that other tree and come back. It doesn't look strong enough to take three."

Once Ben and Badger were safely up, the others crossed the few yards to the other tree. Will helped the girls up before rushing back to join Ben and Badger.

They were just in time. By the time they had reached safety in the branches, both crocodiles had arrived at the bottom of the respective tree trunks and raised their great heads to look up into the foliage above. As they did so, they emitted the most spine-tingling, blood-curdling hissing sound – a sort of high-pitched clearing of the throat – that expressed a mixture of anger and delight at the prospect of a tasty meal. It sounded rather like this: *Gghhharrreugh!* You didn't need to be an expert to know this sound was intended to terrify the wits out of anyone who heard it.

The tree the two girls were sharing was not quite as big as the one in which the boys were perched, and it had fewer branches. This meant they were only just out of reach of the crocodile below. This seemed to infuriate the beast, which lunged upwards, its great jaws open to reveal a set of vicious, razor-sharp teeth. Both Poppy and Fee curled their legs upwards, hugging the branch they were sitting upon, hoping that it would not bend under their weight and deliver them to the hungry predator below. Fortunately, it was firm enough and the crocodile dropped back, disappointed at having so narrowly missed its prey. But it knew there was time: it had chased prey up trees many times before and had all day to wait until exhaustion caused its victims to tire and lose their grip. Crocodiles are patient creatures; they think nothing of lurking immobile in the water for hours on end, with only the tip of their snouts giving away their presence, waiting for some unfortunate creature to come along.

Will called out from the neighbouring tree. "Are you two all right?"

"I think so." Poppy shouted. "As long as this branch holds out."

Then Fee shouted at the top of her voice, "How

long will we have to stay here, Will? When will the crocs go away?"

Like so many awkward questions, this one hung in the air unanswered for a while. At last, Will replied, "It could be some time."

"Just hang on!" Badger shouted across. "Help will be on its way."

"Did you hear that?" whispered Fee to Poppy. "Badger says help is on its way."

Sometimes, when everything looks hopeless, it is tempting to think positively. Poppy realised that that was what Badger was doing, but what he had said was no more than wishful thinking. "I can't think how he knows that," she said to Fee. "We're miles from anywhere, and even if Mr Rigger came to look for us, how would he know where to start? We're a long way off the track now."

"We could try shouting," suggested Fee.

Poppy looked doubtful. "There's nobody to hear us," she said. "We could shout until our lungs collapsed and it would make no difference."

Fee was silent. Then she said, "What if we got some sticks from the tree and managed to put them in the crocodile's jaws to stop them closing them and biting us?"

Poppy smiled. "I don't think so, Fee," she said. "If we got anywhere near those creatures it would be *snap*! and that would be the end of us."

"What is it?" asked Badger
"A croc!" said Will. "There's a creek full of them over there."

"Just hang on!"
Badger shouted across.
"Help will be on its way."

A similar conversation was taking place in the other tree, where Badger had come up with an idea that he was trying out on Will and Ben. "You see the grass round here," he said, pointing at the expanse of grass and reeds that surrounded the trees.

Will looked at him wearily. "Yes, I see the grass. It's just grass, you know. There's lots of it."

"It's very dry," said Badger.

"Yes, it's dry," Will agreed. "But so what?"

"Dry grass can catch fire," said Badger.

Will said nothing at first. Then he realised what Badger was driving at. "Of course, burning grass would drive the crocs away … Yes, I see what you mean." But almost immediately he shook his head. "We can't start a bush fire, Badger. It's … well, it's just one of the worst things you can do. They can easily get out control and cause a lot of damage."

"I know," said Badger. "But this would just be a small fire. We're surrounded by rivers and creeks, and the sea's not too far away. There's not much room for a fire like that to spread."

"You can never be sure," objected Will. "Bush fires can even jump over water – everybody knows that."

Badger defended his plan. "But surely it's all right if it'll save your life," he said. "If it's the only way we can save ourselves, nobody would blame us."

But Ben suddenly thought of a problem. "Has anybody got any matches?" he asked. "It's all very well to talk about starting a fire, but has anybody got any matches?"

There was silence.

"I haven't," said Will.

"Neither have I," said Badger.

"So I don't see how we could start a fire anyway," added Ben.

Then something occurred to Badger. He had seen a film about how to make a fire without matches. You rub two sticks together, using a small string bow to turn one of them. This can create enough heat to set tinder alight. Or you can concentrate the sun's rays through a magnifying glass over some dry leaves and eventually set them alight. But if none of them had matches, then they were very unlikely to have string or a magnifying glass either.

As he was thinking about this, Badger noticed the binoculars that Ben had slung around his neck. They contained powerful lenses that perhaps could be used like a magnifying glass to start a fire.

"Ben," he said quietly, "could you let me have your binoculars?"

Ben wondered why Badger should want to look through binoculars at a time like this, but he passed them over without comment. Badger took them and immediately began to unscrew one of the lenses.

"Careful," said Ben. "Don't drop them …"

He did not finish. Just as he was issuing his

warning, Badger somehow fumbled his grip of the binoculars. One second they were firmly in his grasp; the next they were falling through the air to land with a thud right next to the crocodile. But the huge reptile appeared not to notice, and after a minute or two he moved his tail slightly, bringing it directly over the binoculars, hiding them completely from view.

Ben gasped and looked at Badger angrily. It is easy to get cross with other people when they do something foolish, but it is important to remember that everybody – and that means absolutely everybody – has made a mistake at some point in their lives. And once you remind yourself of that, it is easier to control any feelings of anger you might have.

"Oh, no," cried Badger. "I'm sorry, Ben. I'll try to get them back."

"No, you won't," Will cut in firmly. "You wouldn't last a second down there."

The three boys were silent. The sheer awfulness of their situation was beginning to sink in: there they were, trapped by two of the most dangerous creatures on Earth. In due course, night would fall and what would happen then? Most people can stay awake late, perhaps as late as midnight, but eventually tiredness creeps up on you, making it more and more difficult to keep your eyes open. Drowsiness builds up, your muscles relax and you drift off to sleep. If that happened to Fee, Poppy, Ben, Badger and Will, they would lose grip of the branches, and the consequences of that were too terrible even to think about. They simply could not allow themselves to go to sleep.

It was now after midday. Overhead, the sun had reached its highest point and had begun its slow journey back down to the horizon. Will knew that they had about six hours of daylight left before nightfall. Looking down at the crocodile at the bottom of his tree, he wondered what was going on in the creature's brain. He had been told that crocodiles did not have a large brain – that the crocodile skull was mostly bone. That might be true, he thought, but they were still capable of showing exceptional cunning in the way they hunted their prey. The crocodile probably knew very well that whatever climbed a tree was bound, sooner or later, to come down – driven by the desperation of thirst or the pangs of hunger, or brought down by the force of gravity when the task of holding on to a branch became too much. So the crocodile must know he would eventually win if he simply sat it out. And why would he not do that? He had nowhere else to go and not much else to do. Sitting at the bottom of a tree waiting for your next meal is a perfectly good way of spending your time if you are a crocodile.

Will wondered whether he might be able to divert the crocodiles' attention in some way. When he had run for the sanctuary of the tree he had been wearing the backpack containing the medicines. He still had that with him, and he wondered whether he could throw it into the grass near the crocodiles. If they saw a large object falling from the tree, they might think it was something edible and slither off to investigate. That would give Will the chance to slip down the tree and run off for help. There was always a risk that the crocodiles might pursue him, but if they were busy investigating the backpack, he might just have the headstart needed to get away.

He explained his idea to Badger and Ben.

"But what if they just ignore the backpack?" asked Badger. "What then?"

Will shrugged. "No harm will be done," he said. "If they pay no attention, then we stay here."

"And that means we die," said Ben.

The other two boys looked at him. "Don't say that, Ben," replied Badger. "Don't give up."

But Ben was struggling. He wanted to be brave; he wanted to act as if he were not afraid, but it was difficult. He knew, though, that he had to try. Mr Rigger had once said to him that if people start to go to pieces when they're in a tight spot, it only makes matters worse. "I'm sorry," he said. "I haven't given up. We'll get out of this – I'm sure we will."

His positive tone almost convinced him, but there was still a tight knot of fear in his stomach. He said nothing more and managed a smile.

Will grinned in return. "Just think of the story we'll be able to tell everybody," he said. "Not many people can have been trapped up a tree by a salty."

Just as Will was saying this, Ben noticed something out of the corner of his eye. When he realised just what it was, he almost fell out of the tree with surprise.

"Look," he shouted. "Henry!"

CHAPTER
14
Henry to the rescue

Henry was at the edge of the grass surrounding the trees, walking slowly, as if he were not quite sure where he was going. His tail, though, was wagging enthusiastically, a little black aerial sticking up confidently behind him.

Badger was excited at first, as Henry's arrival might mean that rescuers were not far behind. But then he remembered that Henry was officially lost and that there would be nobody with him.

Ben's first thought was concern for the dog. Like all dogs, Henry had a powerful sense of smell, and it would not be long before he caught their scent and worked out where they were. And once that happened, he would be in as much, if not more, danger as they themselves were.

"Are crocodiles afraid of dogs?" Ben asked Will.

Will shook his head. "No, I'm afraid not. Crocodiles love dogs," he said before quickly clarifying himself, "I mean, crocodiles love *eating* dogs."

Ben looked over towards Henry, who was now

looking directly towards the trees. "He knows we're here," he said. "Oh no, look ..."

Henry's walk had become a trot, and he was now running straight towards the trees, his tail wagging even faster at the thought of being reunited with his friends.

By now Poppy and Fee had seen him too.

"Have you seen Henry over there?" Poppy called out.

"Yes," shouted Will. "We must try and warn him. Those crocs will be after him once they smell him."

"Henry!" Poppy called out. "Henry! Stop!"

Henry suddenly stopped in his tracks. This was not because he had heard Poppy shouting but because his nose had now told him of the presence of the crocodiles. For a few moments he stood stock still, even his tail now immobile. Then he lowered himself in the grass and began to creep up towards the reptiles.

"What's he doing?" asked Fee.

"I think he's stalking them," answered Poppy.

"But they're much bigger than he is," said Fee. "And their jaws are much more powerful than his."

"I know," said Poppy. "But what can we do?"

There was nothing that any of them could do, so they all watched with bated breath. Nobody said anything until Will muttered under his breath, "I don't believe it – I just don't believe it."

As Henry approached his quarry, the crocodiles

suddenly stirred. They could not see very well through the thick grass, but when they eventually spotted Henry the effect was immediate. Slowly they rose, pulling their heavy bellies and tails off the ground as their small, clawed feet extended for movement. Then they began to move towards him, their bodies making a strange swishing sound as they moved through the grass.

Up in his tree, Ben caught his breath. He could hardly bring himself to watch what was happening. Henry stood no chance, he thought. There would be a dreadful moment when the first of the crocodiles got to him, then the whole thing would be over in a second.

But Ben was wrong. Henry was not a foolish dog – he knew very well that crocodiles were deadly dangerous. He understood too that if he attracted their attention, these great scaly creatures would be unable to resist the temptation to snatch a ready meal of delicious dog rather than wait for a less tasty people-snack to drop from a tree. As well as being intelligent, Henry was brave, and like any brave dog he was ready to take a risk if he felt his human friends were in danger.

Henry inched forward, the hair on the back of his neck raised in a tight, prickly ridge. As he moved, he growled, baring his teeth in defiance. Of course, his teeth were nothing compared with those of the crocodiles – great, yellowing fangs, each one capable of inflicting a terrible wound on whatever unfortunate creature came into contact with them.

As Henry moved forward, so did the crocodiles, and now there was barely any distance between them. Poppy held her breath; she could hardly bear to look at what she thought would be the inevitable result of this mismatched encounter.

Suddenly one of the crocodiles lunged forward, snapping its jaws in the air as it sought to cover the remaining ground between it and the growling dog. Had Henry been at all slow, that would have been the end of him. But he was not. Leaping up with a yelp, he turned tail and ran, pursued by the two angry crocodiles. He was much faster than they were, and as soon as he had reached a safe distance he stopped to look back at his pursuers, before running off again, all the while drawing the crocodiles further and further way from the trees.

Will knew instinctively what they had to do. "This is our chance," he shouted. "Everybody climb down and follow me."

He did not need to repeat the order. Shaking with a mixture of excitement and relief, Poppy slid down the trunk of her tree. She was soon joined on the ground by Fee, Badger and Ben. Then, following Will, they all ran as fast as they could in the opposite direction from that in which Henry had drawn the crocodiles.

"What about Henry?" panted Fee, glancing over her shoulder to see what was happening.

"He'll be fine," answered Poppy. "He's smarter than those crocs. They won't catch him."

Will led them back to the path. It was getting late now, and he decided that there would not be time to get back to the beach by nightfall. It would be safer, he explained, to make their way to his village. They could go back to the beach the following day, when it would be much safer.

"We'll be fine at my place," he said to Poppy. "We can have something to eat and you can meet my folks."

Poppy said that this sounded like a good idea, and Badger agreed. He was beginning to feel hungry and the thought of having a meal was an attractive one. It was certainly better than *being* a meal for a hungry crocodile.

There was great relief in the village at Will's safe return, and a warm welcome for his new friends too, when they eventually arrived. Although Will knew his way about the bush, the villagers had been worried when he hadn't returned the previous day and had even sent out a search party, which had been unable to find him. There had also been concern about the medicines. Had something happened to the plane that was bringing them? Had it crashed? Fortunately, all these worries could be dispelled.

As well as meeting Will's parents, the visitors were taken to see the head of the village, an old man with a deep voice and a pair of bright, searching eyes. He listened as Will told him what had happened with the crocodiles. "You have to watch those fellows," he said, shaking his head. "You don't get any second chances with them."

Will's mother prepared a meal that included all her son's favourite dishes. After they had eaten, Will showed Poppy, Fee, Ben and Badger around, introducing them to his friends, who listened in both horror and relief to the story of their narrow escape. Then, as the sun slipped below the horizon and darkness embraced the land, Will led them to the house where they would spend the night. This belonged to the teacher at the settlement school, a kind woman who handed each of them a blanket and a pillow and found a spot for them to sleep. Poppy and Fee shared a floor in the storeroom, made comfortable with cushions from her living-room chairs. Ben and Badger slept on the veranda, on a couple of old sofas. From where they lay, they could look up at the night sky – a great field of stars stretching from one edge of the horizon to the other. Ben saw the Southern Cross, a constellation that has guided sailors for hundreds of years. Badger saw a shooting star, a meteorite, tracing a line of silver across the sky. He wanted to draw Ben's attention to this, but exhaustion overtook him and he managed no more than a few mumbled words before his eyes closed and he slipped off to sleep.

Poppy could not get to sleep so easily. She was worried about Henry, whom nobody had seen since he had saved their lives earlier. They had been unable to go back to look for him: that would have exposed them once more to the crocodiles and would have been twice as dangerous in the dark. So they had had no alternative but to leave him behind, hoping that the brave and resourceful dog would be able to look after himself.

"Don't worry too much about Henry," Will said. "I'm sure he'll turn up."

"But what if he gets lost again?" Poppy asked. "He could be lost in the bush forever."

Will had assured her that this was unlikely. "He'll be all right," he said. "Dogs know how to look after themselves."

Poppy hoped that Will was right, but that did not stop her worrying. At long last she fell asleep, only to have dreams in which Henry was in some sort of danger. These dreams were vivid and were made all the worse by the appearance of Hardtack and Shark. In one of them, the two boys were riding on crocodiles, having rigged up saddles and reins to make it possible for them to chase after Henry on the backs of the scaly monsters. It was a bad dream by any

As Henry moved forward, so did the crocodiles, and now there was barely any distance between them.

Ben saw the Southern Cross, a constellation that has guided sailors for hundreds of years . . .

Hardtack and Shark were riding on crocodiles, having rigged up saddles and reins . . .

standards, and when she awoke, just as dawn was breaking, it was with a feeling of relief.

They did not linger over breakfast, but had a quick bowl of fruit and some bread that Will's father had baked. Then they set off to get back to the beach, avoiding the area where they had seen the crocodiles the previous day. If there are some experiences in life that you do not want to repeat, then being chased up a tree by a hungry saltwater crocodile must be high on the list. But although they all felt relieved that they were going back to the *Tobermory*, they were also anxious about what would happen on their return. Would they get into trouble for getting lost in the first place? Would a search party have been sent out? These were just two of the questions they asked themselves as they made the long journey to the beach, where, much to their surprise and joy, not to mention relief, Henry was waiting for them.

"Look!" shouted Poppy, her voice rising with excitement. "There's Henry."

Hearing her cry, Henry turned round and raced over the sand to greet them. Leaping into Poppy's arms, he covered her face with wet dog kisses before wriggling out of her grasp to welcome the others with a similar show of affection. Everybody was laughing – with relief as much as with pleasure. Henry was safe. That was the best outcome anyone could have wished for.

But then they saw the liberty boat, with Mr Rigger

and Miss Worsfold standing beside it, looking far from pleased.

"What on Earth have you been doing? Where have you been?" asked Miss Worsfold. "Don't you realise that everyone's been worried sick?"

For a few moments there was silence. Then Poppy explained. "It wasn't our fault," she said. "We were trapped by crocodiles."

Miss Worsfold let out a gasp. "Crocodiles? You were in the water?"

"Up a tree," said Badger.

Mr Rigger frowned. "Crocodiles up a tree?"

Badger laughed. "No, sir, we were in the trees and the crocodiles …"

"… were at the bottom of the trees," continued Ben. "And then Henry came along and the crocodiles saw him and so we were able to …"

Fee took up the story. ". . . we were able to climb down the trees and run. Then we went to Will's place because by then it was too late to come back here …"

"Because of the crocodiles," Badger chipped in.

"Hold on," said Mr Rigger. "Will somebody please start from the beginning?" He turned to Poppy and she began to recite the full story, incident by incident. And as she did so, Mr Rigger and Miss Worsfold began to understand that nobody had been at fault and that, in fact, everybody had behaved in exactly the way they should have.

"You did very well," said Mr Rigger at the end. "And now I suggest we get back to the *Tobermory*. We've lost enough time as it is."

This meant it was time to say goodbye to Will, which was hard for them all, as he had become a good friend in the short time they had known him. And they knew, too, that if he had not been with them when they met the crocodiles, everything could have turned out very differently. It was Will, after all, who had acted quickly and told them to run for the trees. And it was Will who had then led them to the safety of his village

"I hope we meet again sometime," said Badger, as he shook Will's hand.

"I do too," said Will. "You never know, do you?" He too was sorry to see his new friends go and said that he hoped they would call in if they ever sailed that way again. Then they climbed into the liberty boat and began to row back to the *Tobermory*, with Henry standing up at the prow of the boat, sniffing the air and barking as loudly as he could to let everybody on the ship know that all was well.

Once back on board, Ben, Fee, Poppy and Badger were all summoned to the Great Cabin, where the whole story was told once again. Captain Macbeth listened intently and then, just as Mr Rigger had done, he congratulated them all on keeping a cool head and doing the right thing.

"It's Henry who deserves congratulations," said Badger. "He's the real hero for leading those crocodiles away from the trees."

Captain Macbeth leaned down to pat Henry on the head. "I think you deserve some treats, Henry," he said.

Henry wagged his tail. He recognised a few words, but he certainly knew what 'treats' meant. The Captain reached into the drawer of his desk, where he kept a packet of Good Dog Extra Meaty Treats. Taking a handful of these from the bag, he tossed them towards Henry, who leapt up in the air to catch them in his mouth. Everybody clapped.

Badger was right: Henry had been a hero and had he not done what he had done, then … It was too awful to think about what might have happened, so nobody said anything more about it. They were all back on board the *Tobermory* none the worse for their experiences, and that was what counted.

That evening the Captain addressed the whole school in the mess hall after dinner.

"We shall set sail in an hour," he said, "and try to make up for lost time." He paused. "Are there any questions?"

For a minute or two nobody said anything. Then a hand went up. It was Bartholomew Fitzhardy. "Are we still in the race, Captain?"

Captain Macbeth answered without hesitation. "Of course we are, Fitzhardy," he said.

There was a murmur of dissent from the table occupied by Hardtack and his friends.

"But, sir," said Hardtack, "we've lost so much time. What point is there going on when the other boats will be miles ahead of us?"

"Yes," echoed Geoffrey Shark. "What's the point?"

Badger turned round in his chair and glared at Shark. "We don't *have* to win, Shark," he said. "We stopped because we had to. That's the law of the sea: you have to help people in trouble." He paused. "Even if it means losing a race."

Hardtack did not like this at all. "Speak for yourself, Striped One," he hissed, using one of his favourite nicknames for Badger. "Not everybody's a loser like you."

Mr Rigger, who had overheard this, clapped his hands sharply. "No arguing, please," he shouted. "Any other questions for the Captain?"

When there were none, Mr Rigger announced who would be on the various watches through the night. Ben and Badger were on a watch that would start in the small hours of the morning. Poppy and Fee were on the watch that ended at dawn. This was a popular one, as the people on that watch were allowed to lie in late and have breakfast any time they wanted.

Shortly after, with a great clanking and creaking, the *Tobermory*'s anchor was raised and they set sail in the darkness. From the ship, the coast was just a dark shape, devoid of detail. Fee watched it as it slipped past, thinking about how somewhere in those shadows were the crocodiles that had nearly eaten them. She felt grateful that she was still alive and not in the dark cavern of a crocodile's stomach. This was proving to be an eventful voyage – and a perilous one too. She wondered what further dangers they might still face, but could not think of any. That is the trouble with danger, she thought: it is often completely unexpected . . .

CHAPTER 15
An anonymous note

The following morning, when the *Tobermory* was well out to sea, news came through of the other ships in the race. It was Mr Rigger who received it first, listening in on the radio, and he lost no time in passing it on to the Captain. The Captain told Matron, and Matron told Miss Worsfold, who in turn told Poppy, who told Fee, who told … and so it passed around the ship until, within minutes, everybody knew but despite having lost time, they still had a fighting chance to win.

Up on deck, Badger and Thomas were on helm duty with Amalia, a girl who had joined the ship for this voyage. Amalia went to school in Russia, but had come to spend a term on the *Tobermory*. Badger had been teaching her about steering and how to keep the ship at just the right angle to the wind so the sails worked as efficiently as possible. It was part of the *Tobermory*'s tradition that the more experienced sailors helped those with less experience.

Mr Rigger came up from below deck to check on them.

"We're still in the race," he said, "so see if you can get a few extra knots out of her." Speed on a ship is measured in knots, so a few extra knots could make all the difference as they sailed in the direction of Kangaroo Cliff.

Badger explained to Amalia how the sails would be adjusted, then Thomas called out the instructions to the members of the crew who were tugging on the various ropes that would bring the sails into the right trim.

"I think we're going a little faster," said Amalia. "I can feel it."

Earlier on, classes had been suspended since the *Tobermory* was in a race. Now, because the race was taking longer than expected, some classes had started again. Poppy and Fee were both in a biology class being held by Miss Hedges, a popular teacher who taught general science. Miss Hedges had been explaining how green leaves trap carbon dioxide and release oxygen, and Poppy was writing this down in her notebook when she noticed Amanda Birtwhistle staring at her from the other side of the classroom. At first she tried to ignore her. Ever since the incident with the giant clam, when Amanda had lied to get herself out of trouble, the two girls had not spoken to one another. Now, Amanda was looking at Poppy in a way that she found quite disconcerting.

"Amanda's staring at me," Poppy whispered to Fee.

"Look over there. See? She's staring."

Fee glanced over towards Amanda. "Yes," she whispered back to Poppy. "It's creepy, isn't it?"

"She's trying to make me feel bad," said Poppy, "but *she's* the one who should feel bad. She's the one who lied."

At the end of the class, Poppy waited until Amanda had gone before she herself left the class-room with Fee. There was no sign of Amanda up on deck, and Poppy did not think much more about the matter. If Amanda wanted to ignore her, there was nothing she could do about it. Poppy had plenty of friends, and it would not be the end of the world if Amanda chose not to speak to her. At the same time, of course, nobody likes it if there is a feeling of hostility in the air, and Poppy was no exception.

Then something unexpected happened. Every student on the *Tobermory* had a pigeon-hole where mail or messages could be left and where teachers could return exercise books after they had been corrected.

Poppy went to her pigeon-hole that afternoon to see if there was anything for her. There was an essay she had written for Miss Worsfold, corrected in the red pen that the teacher always used, and there was a note from Matron reminding her that she should collect a fresh bottle of sun-cream that everybody was obliged to use when the *Tobermory* was in hot climates. But there was something else – an envelope with her name written on it and, inside, a single page of notepaper. On the notepaper was written the simple message: *I'm sorry.* There was no signature and no other means of telling who had written it.

Poppy was perplexed. Later that afternoon, when they were off duty and had free time to sit on deck to read or to practise their knots for the knot-tying test that was coming up in a few days' time, Poppy found herself sitting up near the bow of the ship with Badger, Ben and Fee. It was a favourite place for the friends to sit, as there was always a fresh breeze there, accompanied by the swishing sound made as the *Tobermory*'s bow made its way through the water.

Poppy showed her friends the mysterious note.

"Who's sorry about what?" asked Badger, handing the note back after he had examined it.

Poppy explained that she had no idea.

"Perhaps it's a mistake," suggested Fee. "Perhaps somebody put it in the wrong pigeon-hole."

Poppy shook her head. "No. There was an envelope," she said. "It had my name written on it."

Ben looked thoughtful. "What about the hand-writing?" he asked.

They all turned to look at him. "What about it?" asked Poppy.

"Perhaps somebody will recognise it," he said. "After all, everybody's writing is different, isn't it? Even if the differences are small – the way you dot an 'i' or cross a 't', you can still tell." He paused for this to sink in before continuing. "I can always tell if something's been written by Fee. She always puts a bit of a squiggle at the end of every 'w'. Don't ask me why she does it, but she does."

Fee defended herself. "My writing's neater than yours," she said.

"I wasn't criticising you," protested Ben. "I was just saying that that's the way you write."

"There's no need to argue," Poppy interjected. "I think that Ben's on to something. If we can find out whose writing it is …" She stopped. It had suddenly occurred to her that there was an easier way to find out who had written the note, and that was to think of who might have a reason to say sorry to her. And there was only one answer to that.

"Do you have an idea?" asked Fee.

"Yes," said Poppy. "Amanda Birtwhistle. I should have thought of her before."

They all knew the story of the clam incident. Of course Poppy was right: Amanda had every reason to apologise to Poppy, and this must be her way of doing it.

"But why doesn't she just come to you and say sorry?" asked Badger. "If she's sorry, then why not say sorry – like any normal person?"

Poppy thought for a moment. "Shame," she said. "She feels ashamed."

Poppy went to her pigeon hole that afternoon to see if there was anything for her.

On the notepaper was written the simple message:

I'm sorry

Poppy shook her head. "No, there's a difference between feeling ashamed .... and feeling scared."

"You mean scared?" Badger said.

Poppy shook her head. "No, there's a difference between feeling ashamed and feeling scared."

Fee knew exactly what Poppy was talking about. "I remember once when I was really mean to somebody, I felt bad about it afterwards, but I couldn't say sorry because I was too ashamed of myself."

Ben agreed. "Same here," he said. "Maybe it's because it seems somehow to make it worse for yourself. You feel bad because of what you've done and you think you'll feel even more awful if you say sorry. So you …" He shrugged his shoulders. "So you don't do anything and just hope it'll all go away."

Poppy looked at the note once more. "What do you think I should do?" she asked

"Speak to her," said Ben. "Ask her: 'Did you write this note?'"

Poppy seemed unsure. "But she may not have written it," she said. "And if she didn't, I'd look really stupid."

Badger thought that if that was the way Poppy felt, then it would be best to be certain that it was Amanda who had written the note before saying anything. "Once you're sure," he said, "you can go and tell her that if she feels sorry, then she should say so to you – not leave anonymous notes in your pigeon-hole."

Poppy thought about this. She was beginning to feel sorry for Amanda; it must be hard to feel so bad about what you've done yet not to be able to face up to apologising for it. If she found out that it was definitely Amanda who had written the note, perhaps instead of confronting her about it she should just go and tell her that it didn't matter. She thought for a moment, and then said to herself, *No, why should I? If she can't say sorry to my face, why should I say anything to her?*

But a voice within her said, *Really? Are you sure?* And so she thought again, and decided she had a choice.

"What are you thinking, Poppy?" Fee asked.

Poppy opened her eyes. "Nothing," she replied.

This is the answer, of course, that people always give when they really are thinking about something but do not want to say what it is.

Poppy now asked Fee a question. "Who sits next to Amanda in class?"

Fee hesitated. "I'm not sure … Wait a minute, it's Amalia, I think."

"So she would know what Amanda's handwriting is like?"

Fee nodded. "I'm sure she would."

Poppy handed Fee the note. "You know Amalia quite well, don't you?"

"Yes," answered Fee.

"Could you show her this note and see if she recognises the writing?"

Fee took the note and tucked it into her pocket. A short while later, as they were going into mess hall for dinner, she saw Amalia and showed it to her.

"Whose writing is this?" Fee asked.

Amalia answered straight away. "It's Amanda's," she said. "Why do you ask?"

"To solve a mystery," answered Fee.

16
Kangaroo Cliff at last

The next day, Mr Rigger received a warning on the radio that a major storm was approaching. Although the forecast could not say exactly when it would arrive, it was clear that the *Tobermory* would be right in its path. When he heard this, the Captain looked carefully at the charts and consulted Mr Rigger. They were standing near the helm with Thomas Seagrape, who was on helming duty at the time.

"Well, Seagrape," said the Captain, "what would you do if a storm were approaching?"

Thomas had been brought up in the Caribbean and knew all about storms. "I'd look for shelter, sir, if I were close enough to land."

The Captain nodded his approval. "And if you were too far out?" he asked. "What then?"

Again, Thomas knew exactly what to do. "I'd get most of the sails in, Captain," he said, "then I'd leave just a very small amount of sail to keep us steady."

"Well done," said the Captain. "What do you say, Mr Rigger?"

"I'd say that this boy knows his sailing," said Mr Rigger, with a smile.

The Captain pointed to the shore. It was not too far away, and so it would easily be possible to reach it before the storm hit. "It won't take us more than an hour to reach shore," he said. "And according to this chart there's a bay there that'll give us shelter from the north-east, which is where the wind's going to come from."

The Captain showed Thomas a place marked on the chart called Fig Tree Bay. "Steer for this place, Seagrape," he said.

In less than an hour, the *Tobermory* nosed her way between two headlands into a wide, deserted bay. The Captain was now at the helm, and all along one side of the ship a class on how to sound depths was being conducted by Mr Rigger. Each person had a long line, with a lump of lead tied to the end. This line was knotted at various points to mark the fathoms – the units of length used to measure the depth of water – and this made it possible to tell just how much water there was beneath the ship. As the line played out, they could feel the weight of the lead, but when it reached the bottom, it slackened. That gave the depth of the water at that point, which is something you really need to know on board a ship. The last thing any sailor wants is to run aground, and the navigator always has to be careful not to guide the ship into water which is too shallow. Of course, the *Tobermory* had an electronic depth-sounder, but a good sailor has to know how to use simpler, older methods – just in case.

In twenty metres of water they let out eighty metres of chain, at the end of which the great heavy anchor dug deep into the sand on the sea-bed. Putting the ship's engines astern, Captain Macbeth made the ship pull for a few moments against the weight of the chain and the anchor until it was clear that the *Tobermory* had come to a complete stop.

"That's it," announced Captain Macbeth. "We should be safe here when the storm hits."

Because of the danger of sharks again, swimming was not allowed, so people had free time for the rest of the afternoon, right up until it was time for dinner.

As they went into the mess hall, Poppy found herself standing in line close to Amanda. This was her moment, and she seized it.

"Amanda," she whispered. "I found your note."

Amanda looked around. When she saw that nobody could overhear them, she turned to Poppy and whispered back, "I meant what I wrote."

Poppy nodded. "That's all right," she said. "I was going to accept your apology."

Amanda looked relieved. "Thanks," she said.

But Poppy had more to say. "But that's not enough, you know."

Amanda frowned. "What else do you want me to say?"

Poppy was prepared. "I want you to go to the Captain and tell him you lied. I want him to know that what happened was not my fault at all."

Amanda's face registered shock. "I can't," she stuttered. "I can't just go in there and tell him."

"Why not?"

"Because … because …" Amanda's voice faltered.

"Then it's no good saying you're sorry," said Poppy. "It's meaningless."

Amanda stared down at the deck. "I felt so bad," she said. "I was just too scared to tell him what really happened."

Poppy spoke firmly. The line of people was beginning to move, and she knew that they did not have much time to finish their conversation. "Then you're going to end up feeling bad for a lot longer," she said. "It's your choice, Amanda – make a clean breast of it and get it over and done with, or feel bad about it for as long as you're at school on the *Tobermory*. You choose."

After dinner, Mr Rigger announced the rota of watches. There had to be at least five people on deck throughout the night, keeping a look-out for signs of rising wind and ready, at a moment's notice, to take the ship out of the bay if the wind shifted and made their situation dangerous. Procedures were set out: at the first sign of rain and wind, one of those on watch would go down below and wake the Captain and Mr Rigger, who would come up on deck and take charge.

"Be vigilant," warned Mr Rigger. "Storms can blow up in no time at all, and if you don't act quickly you can be in serious trouble. There can be winds of over a hundred miles an hour."

Ben and Badger were on an early watch, along with Tanya, while Poppy, Fee and Amanda were on a watch that started just after midnight. They were to be on duty with Bartholomew Fitzhardy and Maximilian Flubber.

"Oh no," groaned Poppy. "I'm on with Flubber." She did not mention the fact that Amanda Birtwhistle was on the same watch. That, she thought, could be awkward, but at least she and Amanda had spoken to one another.

Badger laughed. "Have fun!" he said cheerfully. "We've got Shark. I'd much prefer to be on watch with Flubber than Shark."

Because they would have to get up just before midnight, Poppy and Fee went to bed early. Poppy had some difficulty getting off to sleep, knowing that a night watch was ahead of her, while Fee, who was tired, did not stay awake long. All too soon, their turn came to go up on deck. Poppy had set her alarm to wake them, and they both climbed out of their hammocks, drowsy and dishevelled, ready for duty.

Fee and Bartholomew took up their position at the bow of the ship. Poppy, Flubber and Amanda were at the helm. Together they decided which direction they would cover: Poppy would look out for anything to stern, Amanda would be in charge of the starboard and Flubber would look after the port side.

Separated from Hardtack and Shark, Flubber proved to be surprisingly friendly. He asked Poppy about her adventure with Will, and he listened wide-mouthed as she told him about hiding from the crocodiles up a tree. "I would've been really scared," he said. "I don't know how you did it. I think I would have shaken so much I would have fallen out of the tree."

Poppy was surprised to hear Flubber say that. She did not think she would ever hear Hardtack or Shark admitting to being frightened.

"I think you would have been fine," Poppy said.

Flubber seemed pleased. "Still," he said, "I'm glad you were all right."

He then offered Poppy and Amanda a piece of chocolate from a bar he had in his pocket. They both accepted, and this made Flubber smile. Poppy thought: *He has quite a nice smile, this boy. See, he can't be all bad.*

It was very quiet for the first forty minutes of the

watch. Then, with no warning at all, a wind arose. It did not start gently, but arrived with a suddenness that nobody had been expecting. First there was just wind, blowing hard and cold, howling loudly as it whipped across the surface of the sea. Then there was rain – a white sheet of water which raced across the deck like a suddenly drawn curtain.

Poppy, who was standing near the helm, was joined by Amanda and Flubber, both of whom were struggling to avoid being swept off their feet by the force of the wind.

"What are we going to do?" shouted Flubber.

"We need to wake the Captain and Mr Rigger," Poppy shouted back. "I'll go …"

She did not finish what she was saying. The force of the wind had suddenly increased and she had to grab hold of the wheel to save herself from being blown away. Flubber and Amanda had to do the same, all three of them hanging on for dear life, their clothes being almost torn by the sheer force of the squall. In such conditions, there was no chance of being able to cross the deck safely and go below to get the Captain and Mr Rigger.

"We'll just have to hang on," yelled Poppy. "Whatever you do, don't let go."

Up at the bow, Fee and Bartholomew had ducked beneath the gunnels – the high sides of the ship – and were getting some shelter there. They could not move either, and would simply have to stay where they were until the storm subsided.

Poppy wondered if the Captain would be woken up by the movement of the boat. He was, but as he came up the companionway and onto the deck to help, he was pushed back by the sheer power of the wind. Like the others, he would be unable to cross the deck without being blown over. He was helpless, stuck where he was until the wind dropped and the wild lashing rain had subsided.

They might have been able to ride out the storm had something not happened that every sailor dreads. The anchor was now taking the full strain. With each gust of wind, the *Tobermory* pulled more and more fiercely against the restraining chain, yanking it back and forth like a great metal whip. The pull of the ship was now just too great for it to remain where it was. With a great heave, the anchor freed itself and began to drag across the sea-bed. The *Tobermory* was now moving.

Poppy saw immediately that the situation was extremely serious. The wind had shifted and was now pushing them slowly but surely towards the rocks at the edge of the bay. Unless they could bring in the chain and manage to move the boat out to sea, they were now facing certain shipwreck.

Poppy thought quickly. The anchor chain was controlled from up at the bow. If she could signal to

Bartholomew and Fee, they would be able to operate the windlass that brought the chain in. But would they be able to see her through the sheets of rain?

Fortunately, they did, and interpreted her frantic hand signals correctly. Crawling to the windlass, Fee and Bartholomew began to wind in the chain. At the same time, Flubber turned on the engine and he, Poppy and Amanda began to struggle with the ship's wheel.

It was hard to control the wheel as the boat was tossed about by the storm. Poppy would never have been able to do it by herself, but together they managed to swing the wheel sufficiently to point the nose of the *Tobermory* out of the bay so it faced the open sea. It was very heavy going, but with the three of them to bring the manoeuvre off, they succeeded. Soon the chain was in and the *Tobermory* was making her way into deeper, safer water. And just as that happened, the storm began to abate. The wind dropped and stopped howling quite so fiercely, and the rain began to ease off. From having been a violent storm, it was now just an ordinary, even if still rather badly behaved, storm.

Captain Macbeth was now able to come out on deck. As he joined the three bedraggled students at the helm, he shouted out praise. "Well done, all of you! Quick thinking!"

Mr Rigger also came up on deck, and he and the

Captain took control of the ship.

"You go down below," said the Captain to his bedraggled crew members. "Change into dry clothing and ask Matron to give you a mug of hot chocolate each. I imagine she'll be wide awake by now after all this commotion."

As they made their way down the companionway, Poppy reached out and touched Amanda on the arm. "You were pretty brave up there," she said.

Then she turned to Flubber and said the same to him.

Flubber thanked her, but said that in his opinion it was Poppy who had really saved the day. "I was only following orders," he said. "And you gave me the courage to do what we did."

Amanda looked at Poppy. "I'm going to speak to the Captain tomorrow," she said. "I made up my mind about what to do when we were battling the storm."

Poppy smiled. "I knew you'd do the right thing," she said, and then added, "Thank you, Amanda."

And it was indeed the right thing. Next morning the Captain listened carefully to what Amanda had to say, and at the end of it he accepted that she was sorry and had learned a valuable lesson about telling the truth. But he did more than that. Calling Poppy in, he told her he was sorry for having misjudged her so quickly. "I think we've all learned something," he said. "Myself included."

As is often the case, the final stage of the race was the most exciting part of all. As they sped towards Kangaroo Cliff, they began to see more of the other ships. There was the *Prince of Hamburg*, her sails tightly and expertly trimmed, her crew poised ready to pull on the ropes that would give the canvas whatever tug it needed to get the most out of the wind. She seemed to be in the lead, although there was not much between her and the next two ships in the race – one of which was the *Melbourne*, the other being the *Tobermory*.

Ben could hardly believe his eyes when he saw they were one of the first three. "I thought we'd lost any chance we had once we stopped to help Will," he said to Badger.

Badger was as surprised as Ben, but he had been speaking to Mr Rigger, who had explained to him what had happened. "Apparently, all the other ships had some sort of incident as well," Mr Rigger told him. "Most of them were caught up in the storm last night. We were lucky – it didn't set us back too much, but others weren't that fortunate and were blown badly off course."

Then there had been medical emergencies on two of the other ships. One was a case of appendicitis, which had required the ship to stop altogether while a surgeon carried out an operation. But there had been complications and the ship had had to divert to a port to drop the patient off at a hospital. That had cost them several days. Sickness had broken out on board another ship, requiring it to remain at anchor for two days whilst the crew recovered.

There were other things too that Mr Rigger had heard over the radio. The New Zealand ship, the *Spirit of Hokianga*, had sprung a serious leak and had spent a few days in a river delta while her hull was patched up. Then the Russian ship had lost her rudder and had to make, and fit, a temporary one before she could continue. All these misfortunes meant that in the final leg of the race the *Tobermory* now stood as good a chance as any of winning.

The first sighting of Kangaroo Cliff was made by Tanya, who was on watch with Amanda up in the crow's nest. When she shouted the news to the others, a great cheer arose from everybody on deck.

"We'll be there in no time at all," shouted Ben.

"And we've got a good chance of winning," shouted Badger. "Look – we're right with the front-runners."

"I told you never to give up," said Mr Rigger proudly. "A race isn't over …"

Badger knew what was coming: "… until it's over," he added.

"That's right, young Tomkins!" exclaimed Mr Rigger. "You seem to know in advance what I'm going to say, but remember, if you have something worth saying then …"

"… then you should always say it," Badger said, with a smile.

"Exactly," said Mr Rigger. "That's exactly what I was going to say!"

Now, with just a very short distance to cover, the race had become a touch-and-go affair. The three leading ships, the *Tobermory*, the *Melbourne* and the *Prince of Hamburg* were neck and neck, spread out in a wide line, each doing much the same speed as the other.

"Do you think it's going to be a dead-heat?" Angela asked, as she stood at the railing with Fee, Ben and Badger.

Fee shook her head. "Somebody will pull ahead at the last moment," she said. "It's going to be close, all right, but there'll definitely be a clear winner."

"I hope it's us," Angela said. "Oh, I do so hope it's going to be us."

It was impossible to say which of the ships would manage to put on that extra burst of speed needed to win. As she looked across at the other two ships, though, Fee noticed there were signs that the *Melbourne* was speeding up. But then, a moment later, the wind shifted a little and the Australian ship slowed down again.

Poppy and Thomas were at the helm for this final

stage, with Captain Macbeth and Mr Rigger standing immediately behind them, calling out orders. Suddenly the Captain seemed to notice something and turned to speak to Mr Rigger. Both of them looked over to starboard, towards the *Prince of Hamburg*. There was no mistaking the look of shock on both their faces.

"Poppy and Thomas, Mr Rigger will take the helm now," said Captain Macbeth urgently, as he unfurled a chart and examined it closely, the paper flapping wildly in the wind. Once again he conferred with Mr Rigger. Nodding his head to confirm the order the Captain had given him, Mr Rigger swung the wheel over to starboard, making the ship turn sharply, right into the path of the German boat.

Fee was astonished. "Why is he doing that?" she asked.

Her question was directed at nobody in particular, and for a moment it hung in the air before being answered by Badger.

"I think he's trying to get the *Prince of Hamburg* to swerve," he said. "And look – that's exactly what's happening."

Faced with the prospect of the *Tobermory* straying into its path, the German ship had no choice but to turn as well. This change of direction took it slightly further out to sea, ending its chances of winning. But the *Tobermory*'s manoeuvre also put paid to any hope

The great heavy anchor dug deep into the sand on the sea-bed.

Then there was rain – a white sheet of water racing across the deck like a suddenly drawn curtain.

SCHOOL SHIP TOBERMORY

Mr Rigger swung the wheel sharply over to starboard, making the ship turn sharply, right into the course of the German boat.

of victory for that ship. With her two rivals out of the running now, the *Melbourne* cruised decisively into the lead to win first place. The *Prince of Hamburg* was second and the *Tobermory* third.

There was no hiding the disappointment Captain Macbeth's crew felt. It had been so close, and had it not been for the Captain's odd change of course at the last minute there would have been a perfectly good chance that they would have won.

That thought was uppermost in the minds of all the students as they waited to be addressed by the Captain. They had now dropped anchor in the bay in front of Kangaroo Cliff and were waiting to have the debriefing that every crew has at the end of a race.

"The first thing I'd like to say," Captain Macbeth began, "is well done! Coming third in a race like this is a very good result, and I think you can all be proud of yourselves."

His words were greeted in silence. It might be true that third place was not a bad result, but how much better it would have been to be second, or even first – and both those results had been within their grasp.

The Captain looked out over the heads of the students. Under his breath, he muttered to Mr Rigger, "I know how they feel."

The Captain cleared his throat. "You'll be wondering about what happened towards the end," he said. "Well, I've just been on the radio to the captain of the

Prince of Hamburg and I've explained to him why I forced them to change course."

The whole ship's company was listening attentively. There was not a sound to be heard other than the noise of the wind in the rigging.

"I'm glad to say that the German captain completely understands," continued Captain Macbeth. "And more than that – he thanked me for doing what we did."

Badger looked enquiringly at Ben. "Have you got any idea what this is about?" he asked.

Ben shook his head. "None at all," he replied. "Let's see what he says."

Now came the explanation. "Just before I ordered Mr Rigger to turn to starboard," said the Captain, "I realised the *Hamburg* seemed unaware of some submerged rocks directly ahead of her. Had she hit them, she would have been seriously damaged and probably would have sunk."

Ben held his breath. "So that explains it," he whispered to Badger.

The Captain continued. "They were so busy racing that I don't think they had consulted their charts. We could have tried to contact them on the radio to warn them, but we didn't have time. And there might have been nobody in their radio room anyway."

Mr Rigger, who had been standing next to the Captain, now took over. "The Captain did the right thing," he said. "We had to save them from disaster, even if it meant losing our chance to win the race. And the only way we could do that was by forcing them to turn."

"I know it's disappointing," continued the Captain. "I'm disappointed; Mr Rigger's disappointed; the whole ship's disappointed. But ..." He paused, looking directly at the students standing before him. "But if there's a choice between doing the right thing and winning a race, then I'm in no doubt whatsoever which you must choose." He paused again. "Does everybody agree with me on that?"

They did.

"In that case," said the Captain, "time to celebrate coming third. Cook has prepared some special ice cream, and I don't want to keep you from that any longer."

A cheer went up for the Captain from the entire crew, who shouted at the top of their voices. They were proud their ship had a captain like Captain Macbeth and that they had the honour of serving under him.

The race was over, but not the trip. There was still the long voyage home, which took them all the way across the Pacific, through the Panama Canal and back across the Atlantic. All the while they were sailing, they had their normal lessons; all the way across the long miles of empty ocean they learned more about how to sail, how to cope with every sort of sea condition. They also continued to learn about many other things – how to get on with people, how to make friends, how to become braver, stronger and more confident.

At last they sailed into Scottish waters and started the final leg of their journey – up through the Sound of Mull towards the colourful town of Tobermory itself. As the ship dropped its sails and came into harbour, a ferry that was taking on passengers sounded its horn in their honour. On the shore there

were people waving, and a Scottish piper, wearing a kilt, greeted them with a bagpipe tune that had been played for many years to welcome people home.

Now it was time for school holidays, and the crew of the *Tobermory* would all be making their way back to their parents or relatives for a month's break.

"I'm going to miss you, Badge," said Ben, as they packed their kit-bags.

"Me too," said Badger. "But it won't be for long."

Badger was right. Before they knew it, they would be back together, ready for the next adventure on board the School Ship *Tobermory*. Nobody knew what that would be, but it's better that way – surprise is an important part of any adventure. And when it is shared with a friend – or even better with a whole crew of friends – then that is the best adventure of all.

If you have enjoyed this book, why not read other School Ship *Tobermory* adventures?

SCHOOL SHIP TOBERMORY

Ben and Fee MacTavish are off to a new school. But this is no ordinary school – it's the School Ship *Tobermory*, where young people from around the world train to be sailors and learn about all things nautical.

When a film crew unexpectedly arrives, Ben is one of the lucky ones to be chosen as a movie extra. But his suspicions are soon aroused – are the director and his crew really making a film, or are they up to something sinister? Ben, Fee and their friends decide to investigate.

ISBN: 978 178027 343 3
£6.99

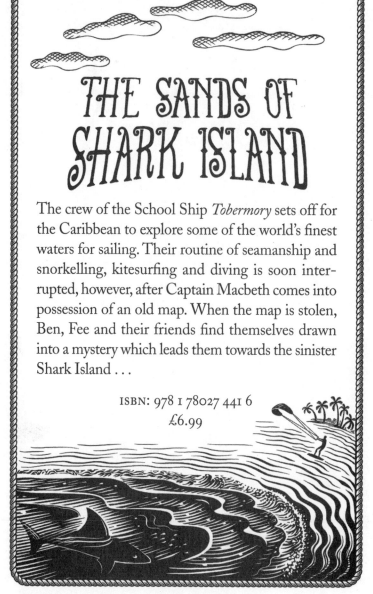

THE SANDS OF SHARK ISLAND

The crew of the School Ship *Tobermory* sets off for the Caribbean to explore some of the world's finest waters for sailing. Their routine of seamanship and snorkelling, kitesurfing and diving is soon interrupted, however, after Captain Macbeth comes into possession of an old map. When the map is stolen, Ben, Fee and their friends find themselves drawn into a mystery which leads them towards the sinister Shark Island . . .

ISBN: 978 1 78027 441 6
£6.99